PRAISE FOR THE NOVELS OF T. A. BARRON

The Mirror of Merlin

"Young sorcery fans, I know this is asking a lot, but I want you to set aside Harry Potter and pick up Merlin. That is, pick up *The Mirror of Merlin*. . . . The writing is taut yet filled with rich images, sophisticated allusions to Celtic folklore, and surprising touches of humor."

—*The Cincinnati Enquirer*

"With lots of surprises and some laugh-out-loud humor to leaven the palpable feeling of doom, this should be eagerly devoured." —*Booklist*

The Fires of Merlin

"With each book, Barron's *Lost Years of Merlin* saga just keeps getting richer in characterization, ambience, and Celtic lore. . . . Fans will definitely be clamoring for more."

—*Booklist*

The Seven Songs of Merlin

"Full of action and excitement, but foremost a tale of the heart . . . Merlin's inner journey is convincing and heartwarming. A rich and resonant read." —*Kirkus Reviews*

The Lost Years of Merlin

"In this brilliant epic, T. A. Barron has created a major addition to that body of literature dealing with the towering figure of Merlin . . . Barron combines the wellspring of mythical imagination with his own deepest artistic powers. An intense and profoundly spiritual adventure." —Lloyd Alexander

"A novel rich with magic."

—*The New York Times Book Review*

TREE GIRL

T. A. BARRON

ACE BOOKS, NEW YORK

TREE GIRL

An Ace Book / published by arrangement with
the author

PRINTING HISTORY
Philomel Books hardcover edition / 2001
Ace digest edition / October 2002

Visit our website at
www.penguinputnam.com
Check out the ACE Science Fiction & Fantasy newsletter!

ISBN: 0-441-00994-8

ACE®
Ace Books are published by The Berkley Publishing Group,
a division of Penguin Putnam Inc.,
375 Hudson Street, New York, New York 10014.
ACE and the "A" design
are trademarks belonging to Penguin Putnam Inc.

PRINTED IN THE UNITED STATES OF AMERICA

10 9 8 7 6 5 4 3 2 1

for

Denali and Larkin,

my tree girls

Chapter 1

"SHE DANCED WITH ME, SHE DID."
Anna narrowed her hazel green eyes, and nodded at the squirrel beside her on the branch. "Danced for hours—aye, even into the night."

But the squirrel, busy chewing on a fir cone, just ignored her. And kept munching. All the while, its tail licked the air like a furry tongue.

Anna laid her hand on the trunk of the tree, the great fir she called Old Master Burl. Then she gave the branch a bounce. It creaked as it rocked both herself and the squirrel. She closed her eyes. And for a thin sliver of a moment, she wasn't in that tree at all, but in her mother's arms, swaying to a dance she could barely remember.

From a time she could barely remember.

With the mother she could barely remember.

"And she sang to me, too," said Anna dreamily. "A song all soft and slow and whispery. A song that blew like the wind . . . aye, and beat like a heart."

She bounced the branch again—this time so hard, the squirrel dropped its cone. With a burst of angry chatter, it scampered up the trunk. Bits of bark rained down on Anna.

"Flying fish eggs," she muttered. She pulled a sticky wad of sap out of her hair. "Look what that little beast did to me, Burl!"

She gazed up at the tree and filled her nose with the familiar smell of fir, both tart and sweet. She didn't need any answer. Not from Old Master Burl. She just knew he heard every word she said—sometimes before she said it.

A few hairs came off with the sap. Anna turned them slowly in her hand. The day's last light caught them, and they gleamed as golden brown as summer squash. What color, she wondered, was her mother's hair? And was it long, so long it swayed whenever she danced?

Suddenly she heard a sound. Aye, a pitiful sound, halfway between a squeak and a whimper. *Cheeeyup. Cheeeyup.*

Anna spun around, searching for whatever had made it. There—it came again, from the roof of the cottage that stood beside Old Burl.

She slid down the branch and leaped onto the roof.

Her knees, covered with leggings she'd woven from strips of sea kelp, crunched into the thatch. But just as she landed, the branch sprang back and swatted her right on the bottom.

"Now, Burl," she scolded. "Remember your manners!"

A wind rustled the fir's needles, and the whole tree seemed to shiver with laughter. Anna herself couldn't keep from grinning. How could she stay angry? She liked Old Burl's pranks as much as he did.

Using both hands, she grabbed hold of the brittle thatch and climbed up the side of the roof, all the way to the ridgepole. She stood there, on the very top, feeling tall. Tree tall. Like Burl's own little sister! Her grin widened.

On one side of the cottage, she could see the wide ocean, striped with rolling waves. On the other side, she could see the dark forest, whose branches moved with waves of their own. Endless water on her left, endless woods on her right. And in between, the narrow strip of rock and sand and sea kelp that was her world, her home.

And the home of Master Mellwyn, who had built this cottage for them both.

Anna's grin faded like a footprint in the sand. The

master had changed—sure as sea foam. She didn't have to be nine years old to see that. And their life together had changed, too. Something was missing now. Something she needed.

But what? He hadn't hurt her. Or grumbled any more than usual. And he always shared his fish, even if the catch wasn't hardly worth cooking. And no matter how far he ranged on the ocean during the day, he always came back to the cottage at night—except for the one night of the year he sailed to the Farthest Reef.

What was it, then?

Anna gazed out across the lagoon and the open sea, feeling the briny breeze on her cheeks. A pair of dolphins leaped out of the shallows: two gray bodies as sleek as sand dunes. A mother and her child, swimming together.

She swallowed. What she wanted was something more than fish to eat or straw to sleep on. Something the master just couldn't give her. Something even more precious than the friend she often wished for, who would always be ready to climb a tree.

No, what she wanted most of all was . . . a mother. And not just to dance with her, and sing whispery songs. A mother, a real mother, could help her know who she really was. Where she came from.

Where she belonged.

Cheeeyup.

That sound! What in the name of crab claws was it? She stood still on the thatched roof, straining to hear it again. But she heard nothing besides the roll and slap of the sea.

For a while she watched the waves, painted as bright as shells by the setting sun. Then her head turned, as it so often did, toward the forest.

It brought bad luck to look that way, into the very eyes of the forest ghouls. She knew that. And if she somehow forgot, Master Mellwyn never stopped reminding her. But how could it hurt, just this once?

Her back straightened. And she looked, for just an instant, at the forest's dark and shrieking groves. The very places where ghouls lurked. Where they licked their fangs and carved up their prey with bloody claws.

Then she spied the great ridge that rose beyond the farthest edge of the forest. From its folds, as rumpled as a blanket, curls of mist spiraled into the sky. And on top of that ridge grew a single tree—so tall, she could see its shape even from here.

The High Willow. The master had warned her never to watch it, whether in mist or in moonlight. Or above all in full daylight, sharp against the sky, as she saw it now.

And yet . . .

She watched the High Willow, so tall atop the ridge. And a strange new feeling swelled in her chest. A feeling she couldn't quite name.

Something about this tree spoke to her—aye, called to her. If only she could fly across the forest and go to its side! Touch its bark, its branches. Hear the rustle of its leaves. Mayhaps even climb—

Cheeeyup. Cheeeyup.

That sound again!

Anna shook herself, as if waking from a dream. The cry came again—weaker than before. Whatever made it was hurt, she could tell. Badly hurt. With an effort, she turned away from the tree and toward the sound.

Cheeeyup.

Across the roof, next to the chimney, she spied a small, tattered nest. And inside it, something smaller, barely as big as a clamshell. Something wriggling, and alive.

A baby bird!

"I'm coming," she called, using her best mother bird voice. Then she spread her arms wide, like wings, and balanced herself on the ridgepole. With a flap, she set off, dancing down the rooftop.

"I'm coming, my little one. Flying as fast as I can!"

She gave her arms an extra strong flap. But her balance shifted, and she started to slip sideways. Just then, a sharp breeze stirred Old Burl. One of the tree's branches smacked against her side—and knocked her upright again.

It all happened so fast that Anna didn't seem to notice. Or to realize how close she'd come to falling. She just kept on flapping toward the nest.

When she reached the little bowl of straw, thistledown, and sea grass, she found the scrawniest sparrow she'd ever seen. The bird's gray feathers, stuck with bits of broken shell, splayed every which way. One of his wings looked deformed, bent almost in half. And his slim yellow eye watched her crossly.

"Oh," cooed Anna, "what a right handsome fellow you are."

The little creature just snapped his beak at her.

She gathered up the bird and put him in the pocket of her apron. "Come now, let's go down together. The master will be getting back soon, and he's sure to be hungry." She cocked her head. "Just like you, aye?"

She tried to stroke the sparrow's wing, but got a fierce nip in return. "All right then, little one. I know just what you need. A spot of food, a bit of warmth, and . . ."

She paused, smiling to herself. "And a mother."

Chapter 2

JUST AS SHE REACHED THE EDGE OF the thatched roof, Anna saw a faint shape on the horizon. A shape that came steadily closer.

Master Mellwyn! He rowed his boat across the lagoon, cutting through the dusky purple waves. Strings of kelp hung from the hull like a scraggly beard.

Anna jumped off and dropped to the ground with a thud, spraying sand all around. Her apron flapped against her thighs. From inside the pocket, the sparrow gave an angry squawk.

"There now, little one." She gently patted down the apron. "Your first flight. How did you like it?"

The bird tried to bite her with his tiny beak.

"Oh, I'm glad. You did beautifully, really. Someday you'll be a great flier!" She cocked her head. "You'll be needing a name, though. Whatever should I call you?"

She stroked the bird's crumpled wing. "Aye, a great

flier. One who soars, way above the clouds. Like an eagle."

And so Eagle got his name. Anna scurried about and gathered enough woolly lichen to make him a new nest. Above her, the branches of Old Master Burl stirred in the evening air, almost as if they were laughing. Green needles sprinkled the sand.

Seeing the boat approaching the beach now, Anna rushed inside. She threw the nest on the kitchen shelf, patted down its sides, and set the bird inside. Then she tossed him a slice of leftover mackerel—just as the cottage door swung open.

A bent, graying man strode in. So much sea salt encrusted him that he looked like a walking barnacle. With a grunt, he dumped a fish on the rough-hewn table—the only piece of furniture in the cottage, but for two driftwood chairs.

"A mackerel," said Anna brightly. "You did well today, Master." She tried to catch his eye, but he turned away too soon. So she took the smallest knife from the shelf, poured some rainwater into a bucket, and started to clean the fish.

The old man grunted again. "Well enough, mayhaps, to keep us from starvin' tonight. Thunder and blast, girl! I wonder if 'twas worth carryin' me skillet all the way here, seein' how few viddles ever go into it."

"Oh, but you're a grand fisherman, you are. You just—"

"Crab shells!" he cursed, cutting her off. He struggled to pull off his soggy sweater, flapping his arms and spraying Anna with seawater. At last, he flung the sweater, woven from shoots of dune grass, over the chair nearest the hearth. It dripped on the earthen floor.

The old man sat down heavily in the other chair. One of its legs buckled beneath him. With a fresh spate of curses, he propped the broken chair against the main post of the cottage. Then he seated himself again, grabbed a tangled net of vines off the floor, and started to tie the loose ends.

Anna went back to fixing the fish. She started to sing softly, with no particular tune—something she often did for the master. She felt sure, at times, that her voice pleased him, though he never said so outright.

She sang about cresting waves and long-necked gulls, leaping dolphins and bright blue shells. Then came a song she'd made up long before:

Silver whale, silver whale, swim home to me
For I am your anchor, your windward, your lee.

Wide be your tail, aye—wide as the sea
Silver whale, silver whale, swim home to me.

Seal puppy, seal puppy, glide home to me
For I am your haven, your windward, your lee.
Soft be your nose, aye—soft as the sea
Seal puppy, seal puppy, glide home to me.

Eider bird, eider bird, fly home to me
For I am your landing, your windward, your
    lee.
Wet be your wings, aye—wet as the sea
Eider bird, eider bird, fly home to me.

All of you, all of you, come home to me
For I am your everywhere: I am the sea!
Visit yon shores, aye—mountain and tree
But ever your heart shall return home to me.

While she worked and sang, Anna tapped her bare
feet on the dirt. Every so often, she kicked a leg out
to the side, or even spun a turn. But the master didn't
seem to notice.

After a while, he grunted and cast the net aside.
Stiffly, he stepped over to the hearth. He blew

on the coals, then added some shards of wood. The room warmed, and the wet sweater started steaming.

He reached for his pipe, carved from a chunk of purple coral. Taking some dried kelp from his pouch, he packed it into the pipe, along with an ember from the hearth. After a few puffs of greenish smoke, he turned to watch Anna sing and sway.

At last, he said, "Ye be outside when I came home."

She glanced up from the mackerel. "Yes, sir."

"Ye not be enterin' the forest while I'm gone?"

"No, sir."

He kept watching her, and for an instant his face seemed to soften. "Dancin' on the beach, I'll wager."

Her cheeks flushed a little. "I do love to dance."

"Aye, that ye do. Ye be a-dancin' ever since ye started to crawl." He waved his hand that held the pipe, leaving a stream of smoke. "Right here on this very floor."

Anna nearly grinned. The master's mood had improved. "What was it like, that day you found me in the forest? You've never told me a barnacle about it."

He stiffened. "Nor will I! Don't ye be gettin' curious about the forest, now."

"I-I'm not curious about that." Though her voice warbled like a baby gull's, she added, "Just about where you found me. Where I . . . belong."

"Ye belong right here!" he shouted. "Right here, in this cottage. Nowheres else! Do ye understand?"

She lowered her head.

"Well, do ye?"

"Aye," she said weakly.

"Good." He gave a sharp nod, making gray locks bounce on his forehead. "And don't even think about lookin' closer at yon trees. Them ghouls have no mercy, even for a foolish girl."

Anna just bit her lip and started to lard the skillet.

"Claw ye to bleedin' shreds, they will." He rubbed his knuckles. "Or crush ye, bones and all, with their graspin' feet! Why, I only enter the forest when I truly must, to fetch—"

"A wooden post or some vines for the nets," she finished from memory. "I know, Master, I know." Not seeing his glare, she slid the fish into the skillet and carried it over to the hearth. "You needn't remind me again."

His hand shot out and caught her by the elbow. "Indeed, I do, Rowanna." His gray eyes glowed, and he squeezed so hard, she almost dropped the skillet.

"For the ghouls be a-waitin', jest hopin' ye'll make a mistake."

She shook free and backed away, rubbing her sore elbow.

A spider's web of lines creased his brow. "'Twas nine years ago, Rowanna, when I first came through that forest. When I found ye, barely a babe, all alone—wailin' in the roots of the High Willow."

Anna winced in surprise. "The willow? You found me *there*?"

"I found ye in the forest! Thunder and blast, girl! That's all what matters." His voice fell to something like a sigh. "They got yer parents, that's certain. And I swear by the ghost o' me own mother's grave, they almost got us."

He frowned. "That haunted woods be no place for someone of human blood. No place at all. Ye understand?"

"Yes, sir." Slowly, she turned back to the hearth. But she couldn't keep from wondering at his words. The willow. She'd been found at the willow!

Neither of them spoke again. Anna placed the fish over the fire and tended the coals. Before long, sizzling sounds and tangy smells filled the cottage. Firelight pranced over the walls and the sooty thatch above their heads.

A sudden wind blew open the shutter. When Anna rushed over to close it, one of Burl's branches reached inside and tickled her forearm. But she just pushed it away and latched the shutter. This wasn't the time for pranks. She had something more to say to the master—something she just had to ask.

She looked into Eagle's nest. The little bird was sleeping, though one foot slapped at the air. She set a crust of seaweed cake beside him. Then, returning to the hearth, she flipped the fish and added some sea cabbage and bladder weed. Soon the meal was ready, and she brought it to the table.

For some time, they ate in silence. When Anna poured the master some duneberry ale from his flagon, he barely grunted in thanks. Finally she drew a deep breath and leaned forward.

"Could I ask something, sir? Just one thing? And if you answer, I'll never ask again."

The old man just scowled at her.

She cleared her throat. "What was it like up there . . . at the willow?"

His fist clenched.

"Just tell me a little," she pleaded. "Was there any sign, any at all, of my mo—"

"No!" He pounded the table so hard, it rattled. "All I saw was ghouls out to devour me! Be ye lame in the head, Rowanna? That blasted tree—that whole forest—holds nothin' but death. Do ye hear?" His eyes blazed. *"Nothin' but death."*

Meekly, she nodded. And from beyond the cottage walls came the mournful call of an owl, echoing in the night air.

Chapter 3

EAGLE GREW STRONGER BY THE DAY. Stronger—but no bigger. He looked more like a shrunken milkweed pod with feathers than any kind of bird.

He did grow more adventurous, though. By the time spring's first blossoms appeared and new green needles sprouted on Old Burl, the sparrow had started to strut along the shelf, the table, or Anna's outstretched arm. He began to whistle. And to follow Anna wherever she went, inside or out.

But not to fly. His twisted wing hung at his side, a clump of feathers that dragged beside him. Even so, he never missed a chance to attack whatever object, dead or alive, caught his fierce little eye.

"Bring that back now, Eagle," demanded Anna. She was kneeling over the garden that she had, at long last, coaxed from the sandy soil—after three years of collecting seedlings, bulbs, and tubers from the forest edge. "That's my only garlic clove! Rotting ravens, Eagle! I need it for planting."

The bird paid no heed. Holding the garlic in his beak, he shook it and dragged it away, just as he would a poisonous snake. He writhed on the sand, kicking ferociously, beating at his foe with his good wing. Sometimes he'd give a savage whistle, barely loud enough to be heard over the tumbling waves of the sea.

Anna couldn't help but smile. "It's that warrior in you, aye. Well, all right, then. Might I have it *after* you've killed it?"

Eagle paused in his scuffle. Without releasing his prey, he turned a yellow eye on the girl. His head bobbed, almost a nod.

"Good," she replied. "I'll tend to these onion bulbs, then."

Her hand reached into the basket she'd woven from supple stalks of kelp. She plucked out a tiny green bulb and packed it into the soil. Then, without looking up, she reached for another one.

This time she felt nothing but air. The basket was gone!

She sat erect. Where could it have gone? It had just

disappeared, sure as sea foam. Suddenly she spied it—resting on a rock at the edge of the forest.

"Now, that's odd." She glanced over at the fir tree she knew so well. But no, even the long branches of Old Master Burl couldn't reach that far. Strange! And she'd felt only the mildest wind.

Puzzled, she stood up and walked over to the basket. Just for good measure, she gave Old Burl a stern glance. But the tree merely shrugged, dropping a cone on the beach.

The basket sat alone on the rock, shaded by a young oak tree just starting to leaf out. And none of her supplies had been disturbed: She found all her seeds of carrots, red cabbage, radishes, and cauliflower, plus her root cuttings of sea kale and the rest of her onion bulbs. She cocked her head, wondering—then heard something new. It was a faint rippling sound, almost a laugh. And it came from somewhere in the thick tangle of trees beyond the oak.

She looked into the forest, but saw nothing strange. "*Hmmm*. Probably just a squirrel playing tricks."

Shaking her head, she fetched the basket and went back to work in the garden. By midday, she'd planted everything, including the garlic that had been slaughtered by Eagle. She watched a lone crab scuttle past the garden's edge, then stretched out on the sand, her hands behind her head. A salty breeze swept in from the sea. Eagle hopped over and sat in the shade of her leg.

She watched the streaming clouds overhead and tried to find shapes—a scallop shell here, a frond of kelp there. But the shapes kept stretching themselves into trees. Tall and slender, wispy and full, the trees filled the sky. Just as they filled her thoughts.

One tree in particular. Growing one place in particular. But that was a place she shouldn't go, not even in her mind.

She sat up. Eagle had fallen fast asleep beside her on the sand, his ragged wing serving as his blanket. Right now he didn't look like a warrior. Not at all. If he really could fly, where would he go? And where would she go herself, if only she had wings?

Her throat swelled. She got up and stepped over to Old Master Burl. The fir's gnarled trunk almost seemed to bend her way in greeting. She breathed in that familiar smell, both tart and sweet.

"I know where I'd go," she said softly. "The High Willow."

The old fir shuddered with a fresh gust of wind.

"All right, I know it's far away. And dangerous, too. But something calls me there, Burl."

She dug her big toe into the fallen needles among the roots. "I can't explain it. Mayhaps it's just to climb the highest tree around! Or to get away from here for a while. Or . . . to find some sign of my real parents. My real mother."

She started up. Climbing Burl was never hard, one hand over the next, but this time she felt mainly needles in her face, slowing her down. And sticky sap on her hands, feet, and knees. Before long, though, she reached the top. And peered, her eyes wide—beyond the dark lair of the ghouls, beyond the clacks and groans of countless branches, at the distant ridge.

Rotting ravens. No willow! It was completely hidden by mist.

Anna stared, hoping to pierce the vapors with her very sight. Whatever the master would say! Even if she couldn't see the High Willow up close, she had to see it now, from afar. Just had to.

Yet the more she looked, the more mist gathered. Her eyes watered from so much staring. By the sea and stars, that tree just wouldn't show itself! Finally, she climbed back down. Old Burl's branches seemed to stroke her shoulders. But she hardly felt their touch.

On the ground again, she glanced up at the whispering boughs. "I know, I should think of a song. Aye, something full of cheer—to sing for Eagle when he wakens."

She frowned. For there was no music in her head. Just the endless slapping of the sea. She turned toward her little garden—then stopped, rooted like a tree herself. Her basket was gone again!

She whirled around, scanning the shoreline, the cottage, and the dark edge of the woods. No basket anywhere.

Suddenly she spotted it. Right where she had rested on the beach just moments before! She squinted, for there was something even more strange. The basket was standing upside down, balanced on its handle, next to the sleeping bird. And it was shading him from the sun, like a hat held above him.

Or, she realized, like something else: a tiny tree, sprouting from the sand.

Chapter 1

WEEKS PASSED. ANNA'S FIRST radishes poked out of the ground. And wrinkly leaves, softer than thistledown, sprouted from the branches by the forest edge. Aye, and how she loved to rub them on her cheek as she danced down the beach, kicking up sand!

But none of this meant as much to Anna as her growing desire to see the High Willow. To touch it with her eyes, since she couldn't with her hands.

At least once a day, sure as the turning of the tide, she climbed Old Burl. Of course, she always waited until the master had finished his morning grumbles, eaten a slab of smoked fish, and lugged all his nets and gear to the boat—looking like a hermit crab with too big a house on his back. Then, after his rowboat had slipped into the lagoon and dropped over the horizon, she did what he'd forbidden: She climbed those branches. And looked to the far ridge.

To the tree where she'd been found.

Sometimes she saw what looked like an uplifted branch, poking through the mist. Or a faint hint of green. Or a shadowy shape behind the clouds.

But she never saw the whole tree. Not once.

Flying fish eggs, that was annoying! And something else bothered her, too. Something strange. Odd things kept happening, just as odd as her upside-down basket, or that rippling laughter from the woods. And just as hard to explain.

First came her sandals. She'd set them out to dry in the sun after a walk in the shallows to collect a few sea urchins. Then, a moment later, the sandals were gone! They had simply vanished from the beach.

Losing her sandals, by itself, didn't bother her much. She usually walked barefoot anyway. It was the *strangeness*. The mystery of it all. And the mystery clung to her like pine sap to a beetle's back.

Then came the day when she spotted some rowan leaves—a whole bunch of them—growing out of a spruce tree at the forest edge! Now *that* was strange. So strange, she couldn't resist stepping over the bramble bushes that bordered the woods, just to get a closer look.

She blinked in surprise. The rowan branch had

been spliced onto the spruce! Aye, by someone with clever hands. And a sense of humor, too.

On another morn, the sea looked as calm as a wide blue eye, staring up at the clouds. Anna spun some turns on the sand, which left a swirl of prints behind. Then she noticed some other marks on the wet sand— marks she hadn't made herself.

On the spot where the master's boat lay at night, she saw a rough circle. And lots of crooked lines. Could it be a face? She moved closer. Suddenly, she started to laugh. It was the face of the master himself! Aye, that it was!

She shook her head, amazed. "By the sea and stars . . . who did this? Not the master, that's certain."

She fell to her knees beside the drawing. And she traced the lines, made by something about the size of her own finger. Was it just chance? The trail of a crab, or some stones jostled at high tide? No—the likeness, right down to the scowl, was just too perfect.

As she often did these days, she glanced suspiciously at Old Burl. The tree just stood there, though, and seemed to ignore her. She narrowed her eyes. If Burl hadn't done it himself, he knew who had.

But who could it be? And was it the same person who'd stolen her sandals?

As if reading her thoughts, the fir tree stirred. Some branches creaked—or chuckled. Anna watched a moment longer, then turned back to the face in the sand.

She lowered her voice and did her best imitation of the master's gruff voice. "Thunder and blast, girl! Why be ye pourin' that sand in me skillet? Be ye lame in the head, Rowanna?"

The face seemed to scowl even more. Behind her, Old Burl chuckled again. As did Anna.

Eagle jumped down from his perch on her shoulder. He landed with a splat on the sand. Then he strutted right over to the master's chin and started to whistle angrily.

"Watch yerself, ye gall-blasted bird!" It was hard to keep going without laughing out loud, but Anna managed somehow. "Or else I'll feeds ye to the fish. Bet yer scrawny old tail feathers, I will!"

At this, Eagle flew into a rage. He jumped onto the drawing's nose and started pecking hard with his tiny beak.

Anna smiled at the little warrior. She gathered him up, despite all the nips to her hand. "It's all right now, my friend. You scared him so much, he won't talk anymore."

Eagle paced across her palm. He didn't seem at all convinced.

"Here you go. A reward for your bravery." She reached into her apron pocket and pulled out an oak leaf wrapped around a sticky slab of honeycomb. She peeled back the leaf, broke off an edge, and offered it to him. But the valiant bird wouldn't turn away from his enemy—who could, after all, just be playing dead.

Anna took a bite of honeycomb herself. She chewed thoughtfully. "All right, then. What if I rub him out? Then you'll know he's really gone."

Eagle chirped several times.

She put the bird back on her shoulder and gave him his bit of honeycomb. Then she reached over to the drawing. But just as she was about to touch it—

A sharp wind gusted. All along the forest edge, trees twisted and groaned, waving their branches. Old Master Burl's lower branches slapped the sand. Suddenly Anna's sunbonnet, woven from willow shoots the spring before, flew off her head.

She leaped to catch it, but too late. The bonnet

spun in the air, then sailed over the brambles and into the forest. It landed on the very tip of the spruce tree's grafted branch.

"Thundering thumbnails!" She bounded after it, jumping over a bramble bush. At the instant she reached the bonnet, though, a new gust snatched it and carried it to an elm tree a little farther into the forest. There it rested, on a lower branch, quivering in the wind.

She swallowed. Then she glanced back over her shoulder at the cottage—and the safety of the shore. Eagle, clutching her shoulder, flapped his good wing anxiously. He tried to whistle, but his beak was fused together from his bite of honey, so he could only make a stifled squawk.

"Hush now," she told the bird. "I don't want to go in there, either. But really, we're still so close to the beach."

Anna turned back to the forest. She peered at the bonnet, sitting on the elm, dappled with sunlight. It was only fifteen or twenty steps away.

Again she glanced at the shore. Then back to the bonnet.

"Took me two months' work to weave that hat," she grumbled. Her fist clenched, squeezing the remains of the honeycomb. "And no silly old wind is going to take it from me now."

She sucked in her breath and stepped into the forest.

Chapter 5

SUDDENLY—A WHOLE NEW WORLD.
Now Anna's feet didn't sink into sand: They
bounced in a bed of fallen leaves. The briny
smell of the sea faded into a zesty mix of resins, blossoms, and rich, wet soil. And the sounds of sloshing
waves and screeching gulls died away, shushed by the
whispers of branches.

But Anna barely noticed. Her bonnet was now just
an arm's length away!

She reached for it—just as a new gust of wind
shook the elm. Rotting ravens! The bonnet flew right
over her outstretched hands, struck a leaning hawthorn trunk, and bounced into the air again. Almost
as if the trees were playing catch! Then her hat arched
over the backs of a doe and her spotted fawn, who
watched with unblinking brown eyes. Finally, it
landed on a huge beech tree that stood even deeper in
the forest.

Before Anna could move, one of the beech tree's

lower branches lifted up and spanked the doe—right on the flank. But the deer didn't bolt. She just tossed her head, nuzzling the branch as she would an old friend. Anna watched, amazed. Then both doe and fawn trotted off lazily into the forest.

Strange, indeed. But she was in no mood to wonder. She wanted her hat! She dashed through a patch of sweet-smelling ferns, straight to the beech tree.

Up she peered, into the branches. They shone silver in the morning light, with bark as smooth as wave-washed stones. And they held her bonnet! The sparrow on her shoulder squawked bravely. She dropped her honeycomb on the ground, reached for a branch, and pulled herself up.

Higher she climbed, just as she'd done so often with Old Burl. In a few minutes, she drew close to her prize. She leaned out from the trunk, bracing herself with one hand, stretching for her bonnet with the other. She reached farther . . . and farther . . .

Got it! Eagle gave a triumphant chirp.

She put on the hat, pulled it down tight on her head, and climbed back down. She jumped from the bottom branch, landing in some moss between the burly roots. With satisfaction, she tapped the bonnet's brim.

Anna turned to go back to the beach. But something made her pause. She gazed all around. What a place this was!

She stood at the very edge of a glade—a hidden meadow of ferns, tall grasses, and spring bluebells. Light shafted through the boughs of the encircling trees. Bees darted from blossom to blossom, while a small butterfly floated like a yellow cloud above the grass.

She stroked her chin. Sea and stars, this world felt so different from her own shoreline world. And also different from what she'd expected. Could bloodthirsty ghouls really live here?

She looked at the great beech itself. The trunk was so wide! Why, it would take five or six people with outstretched arms to reach all the way around. The silvery bark seemed as shiny as the inside of a mussel shell. And then, at the base of the trunk, she spied something else. A black spot—an opening.

She crept closer. Here was a cavern! Big enough for one person, maybe two. She nudged Eagle with the side of her head. "See there? A secret tunnel!"

The bird peered into the darkness of the cavern, shaking his head from side to side.

"Come. Let's have a look."

Eagle whistled in protest.

"Come on, now. Mayhaps there's a secret room in there! With treasure and jewels and things." She stroked his crooked wing. "No one's going to hurt us. And besides, I've got you to protect me."

The sparrow's tiny chest puffed out a little.

And so she ducked into the cavern. It was quiet, very quiet. She heard the echoes of her own breathing, her own heartbeat, inside the wooden walls. In time, she could see thick, black ridges running up the inner trunk. Like vertical roots, or the veins in someone's arm.

She sighed and leaned against the cavern wall. The wood felt warm against her back. And it almost seemed to form itself to her shape, as if she was the water and it was the cup. She liked being held that way. Cozy, it was. Almost as cozy as a mother's arms.

A sudden cry made her jump. It came from just outside the tree! She turned toward the entrance—just as a bear cub bounded into the glade. His brown fur, covered with burrs and clumps of mud, looked as messy as Eagle's feathers. And his lanky legs, oversized paws, and floppy ears made Anna want to laugh.

Just then another bear, with sand-colored fur, bounded over. Without even slowing down, he plowed right into the first bear and knocked him flat. Though smaller and more scrawny, the sandy bear seemed to burst with mischief.

The two cubs started wrestling. Over and over each other they tumbled, flattening the grass of the meadow. The brown one landed on top, but the sandy one twisted away. Then the smaller bear pounced, only to be hurled into a patch of ferns. Back he came again, quicker than a darting minnow. Legs, paws, and furry necks wrapped around each other. Shrieks and growls echoed through the woods.

At last, they broke apart. The brown bear collapsed in some ferns, panting, while the other kept bouncing around, nudging his friend with his nose. The sandy cub clearly wanted to play some more. But the other wouldn't budge.

Anna watched them snuffle and grunt at each other. Oh, what fun to be a bear! Then the sandy cub reared back on his hind legs and made a new sound— rippling, almost like a laugh.

She gasped. It was the same laugh she'd heard before!

The cub suddenly froze, then turned toward the

great beech tree. For the first time, Anna caught sight of his eyes—wild eyes, fiercely wild. They were green, like her own, but darker. They seemed as deep as the forest itself. And they glowed—aye, like a pair of magical moons.

Ears flapping, the bear loped toward the tree. Anna's heart pounded. He was coming straight at her! She shrank deeper into the cavern, holding Eagle's beak closed.

"Quiet, Eagle," she whispered. "Not a sound."

Just before the cavern entrance, the bear stopped. He crouched low and sniffed among the twisted roots. Seconds later, he raised his head. Something was sticking to his tongue. The honeycomb! With a delighted growl, he started to swallow it—when Eagle suddenly broke loose from Anna's grip and whistled angrily.

The bear jumped backward. He spat out the honeycomb. Then, with a snarl, he shambled closer to the cavern.

All at once he thrust his head into the opening. He was nose to nose with Anna! They both shrieked in terror, and their voices rang inside the hollow.

The cub whirled around and dashed off into the forest. His companion in the ferns bounded along behind. And Anna herself ran off—but the opposite way, back to the shore.

Now the glade was empty again, the ferns and spring bluebells lit by slanting rays. Only a small slice of honeycomb, left on the mossy ground, hinted that something strange had just happened.

Chapter 6

IN THE DAYS AFTER THEIR ENCOUNTER in the glade, Anna often wondered about the strange, green-eyed bear.

"He'd play with me, Burl! I'm sure he would." She stood in the shadow of the tree one morning, not long after the master had left for the day's fishing. Her toes tapped against the mossy roots. "And mayhaps . . . he'd be my friend."

The scraggly old fir shrugged. Some needles fell and sprinkled her hair.

"We could run together. Hide from each other. Aye, and climb some trees!"

More needles.

She looked down at the blackened skillet in her hand, which she'd brought outside to wash in the sea. It still smelled of that morning's breakfast: smoked herring and seaweed cakes. She grinned, knowing that was a breakfast the bear might have loved—though he'd probably rather just have some fresh berries. Aye, big ripe ones from somewhere in the forest.

Her mouth turned down. *Somewhere in the forest.* Finding the bear would mean going back there again. Deeper than before, probably. And playing with him would mean going deeper still. Right into the arms of the ghouls!

She shook her head and leaned against Old Burl. "I guess it just isn't easy to find a friend." Her jaw quivered. "Or a mother."

She looked up into the branches. "What really happened to her, Burl? And to me? And where was I born? Did she bring me to the forest for some reason? Or did I just drop to the ground one day, like one of your needles?"

Anna sighed. Nobody could tell her those things. Nobody . . . but the High Willow. And she couldn't go there to find out. Not with all those ghouls in the way.

She patted the fir's trunk, then walked down to the water's edge. A cool breeze lifted off the water and tousled her hair. Eagle hopped on the beach beside her, always on the watch for a surprise attack from a starfish or an oyster shell. His feet left a thin trail of prints on the sand.

She knelt on the beach at the highest reach of the tide. When the next wave arrived, hissing and sloshing, she dipped in the skillet and scrubbed with a small bit of sponge.

"Quit your dreaming," she scolded herself. "You don't have a mother, that's true. But you still have Old Burl. And Eagle, too. And . . . someone else."

Her head turned toward the cottage. The little home built long ago by the master. His sturdy work had kept out so many storms—and forest ghouls. Even on the one night each summer when he rowed out to the Farthest Reef and slept on his boat, and ghouls had come to the cottage and rattled the door, she'd been safe. Thanks to him.

She stood and shook off the skillet. "Aye, someone else—a person, like me."

Anna drew a deep breath. "He's not spry enough to climb trees. But he speaks my own language. And he lives right here."

She walked back to the cottage with the skillet. And a plan.

Over the next few weeks, spring burst into bloom around the cottage. Leaves and vines, needles and flowers, sprouted from the trees at the forest edge. Berries dotted the brambles, and tiny blue flowers as bright as periwinkle shells popped through the sand. Anna's garden looked more leafy by the day, almost a forest itself.

On top of that, waterbirds arrived—all kinds, from all directions. Egrets, gulls, cormorants, ducks, pelicans, and even a huge, stiff-legged crane, landed right on the beach. All day long they strutted down the shore, nibbling at minnows in the tide pools and slapping the air with their wings. From sunrise to sunset they spluttered and squawked and honked at one another. And also at Eagle, who marched among them like a dwarf among giants.

But the greatest change of all happened inside the cottage. It started when Anna made a new pillow for the master, putting the downy feathers she'd found on the beach into a sack of woven grass. And it kept happening when she changed the straw in their sleeping pallets, hung onion and garlic from the main post, cleaned out the hearth, and fixed the driftwood chairs. She patched up the sealskin that held their fresh water. And gathered fresh mint from the stream that flowed out of the forest. She even found a butterfly's cocoon and draped it on the shutter.

At first, the old man didn't seem to notice. Or say

anything if he did. But slowly Anna began to sense a change in him.

He seemed to curse a little less in the evenings, and to linger at the cottage longer in the mornings. He asked her to sing more and more—which she gladly did. Sometimes he gave her the bigger portion of fish, or helped her chop scallops for the sea broth. And once, to Anna's complete surprise, he squeezed her shoulder gently before going out the door.

The cocoon opened. A pink striped lady-of-the-tides climbed out, with wings all wet and crumpled— like newly sprouted ferns. And for several days, that butterfly flitted around the room. It darted over Eagle's head, ignoring all the whistles, and sipped at Anna's bowl of flowers. Once it even landed on the master's ear—and then laughter, right out loud, shook the cottage walls.

Then came a day when the master stayed home from fishing to fix the rotten planks in his boat. Anna worked alongside him. While she gathered the sap from Old Burl's bark and boiled it till soft, he chopped new slats of driftwood with his axe. Then together they fit the wood into the hull and worked the sticky sap all around, plugging any gaps they could find.

This was Anna's favorite part. How she loved the feel of the wood! Even after years of being worn and beaten by the sea, its grain still ran true. And she wondered if each different wood had a special grain of its own. The way different people have footprints of their own.

The old man looked up from the hull. "Sing to me, would ye now?"

And so she smiled, and sang:

Wood on the water, boat on the waves,
Gray gulls a-soaring high:
I am at sea.
Salt on my tongue, wind on my brow,
Endless horizons here:
Now I am free.

When she finished, she ran her fingers along the newly fitted plank. "It's good to work with you, Master."

"Aye," he replied without looking up from the hull. He blew a puff of greenish smoke from his pipe. "One day mayhaps ye'll come fishin' with me. Ye can haul the nets if ye like."

Anna started. He'd never before offered to take her

along in the boat. "Oh, I do like, I do!" She ran to his side and hugged his neck. "Please let me come!"

"All right, girl. When ye be jest a bit older."

She released him and skipped back to her end of the boat. She danced a pair of perfect twirls on the beach, spraying sand against the hull. And another twirl after that, just for good measure. Then, before starting back to work, she smiled at the master. "You're a much better friend than that bear could ever be."

The old man froze. He dropped his chunk of sap and stared at her, his face suddenly as hard as his coral pipe. "Did ye say . . . a bear?"

Meekly, she nodded.

His eyes flashed. "Have ye been goin' into the forest? While I be gone to sea? Tell me the truth, girl!"

"Aye, b-but it was just—"

"None o' yer excuses!" He slammed his hand against the boat. "Or yer lies! I've told ye ten thousand times what could happen in there. Do ye thinks I want to come home someday and find yer carcass in a tree?"

"No, no." A sob bubbled up from her throat. "I don't . . . I mean, it's not—"

"Hush! Ye fool-brained girl, ye'll be me own death,

too." He grabbed a handful of sand and threw it at her. "Now get back inside where ye belong!"

Anna stumbled, sobbing, back to the cottage. She'd ruined everything. Everything!

She slammed the door hard. The cottage now seemed so bare, so empty. For it lacked what she so much wanted.

And what was so wrong about wanting a friend? The master didn't understand. Didn't care! She knew now that the master could never really be her friend. But that didn't have to stop her from finding someone else.

She wiped her cheeks with clenched fists. "I'm going to find that bear again," she declared. "Aye, wherever I must look! Back to the glade. Or the trees beyond. Or even . . ."

She glanced over her shoulder at the open window. "The High Willow."

Chapter 7

THE MASTER STAYED HOME THE NEXT few days, finishing his boat. Though he often grumbled at the slapping sea, he said not a barnacle's worth to Anna. Even so, he kept a close eye on her. And she did nothing to make him suspect her plans.

Finally, on a morning when gulls and cormorants called to the rising sun, he went to sea again. Anna thought about helping him by holding the boat steady while he loaded all his gear. But her sandals were still missing and there were lots of urchins in the shallows. And besides, she just didn't feel like helping.

So she just watched, her feet planted on the sand, as he shoved off. Eagle's own feet drummed against her shoulder.

"Mind ye, girl," the old man called out to her. "Stay out o' those woods! Do ye hear?"

Anna nodded. She heard.

He started to heave the oars. She watched him pull

away. And watched as, minutes later, he vanished over the horizon.

She waited another moment. Then she turned and strode up the beach to the row of brambles at the forest's edge. She paused for a last look back. The branches of Old Burl stirred as if to wave good-bye.

"I'll be back, old friend. Don't worry." But she felt a strange lump in her throat as she said the words.

She stepped over the brambles—and into the forest world. Her feet crunched on dried needles here, sank into soft moss there. "Oh, Eagle, smell! It's so different in here."

The bird, standing on her shoulder like a soldier on guard, just squeezed her skin with his feet.

Meanwhile, new smells flowed over them like an invisible tide. The air was sharp and sweet and musty all at once. Spots of light danced on the branches, side by side with glittering leaves. Anna felt an urge to dance herself . . . yet she couldn't forget all the master's warnings.

Alert. That's what she had to be. Aye, alert and careful.

She noticed then something strange. The forest seemed quieter than before. No branches rustled, no squirrels chattered. No birds whistled at the sparrow on her shoulder. And she had the uncomfortable feeling she was being watched. By someone she couldn't see.

"What is it, Eagle? Do you feel it?"

The bird shifted his weight uneasily.

At last, they approached the glade. There was the great beech tree. And the meadow of flowers, even more colorful than before.

She paused under a twisted pine. Where would be the best spot to wait for the bear? Over there in the cavern of the beech? She chewed her lip. And what should she do if the cub didn't come back to the glade? Despite her vow to find him, she didn't feel ready to go any deeper into the forest. Not yet, anyway.

Thunk! A pinecone dropped on her head, glancing off the brim of her bonnet.

Eagle screeched at the tree, as Anna peered into the thick branches above. She picked up the cone and hefted it in her hand. "Just a little welcome from this old tree," she told the bird. "Probably a cousin of Burl's."

Eagle made an annoyed squawk.

She started to walk closer to the glade, when

thunk! came another cone. This one smacked the middle of her back.

Her eyes narrowed. "That's not very nice of you, tree." A slow grin spread across her face. "Unless, of course, you mean to play toss."

Taking the first pinecone, she heaved it as hard as she could up into the branches. It vanished, with a *swoosh,* into the mesh of needles. Then, a few seconds later, it came back down, gently enough that she caught it with ease. Again she hurled it up into the tree. She waited, but this time the cone didn't come back.

Her grin broadened. "Good catch! Mayhaps we'll play again sometime."

She turned again to the great beech and the glade beyond. Even as she started to walk nearer, another object dropped from above, just missing her nose. It slapped the ground at her feet, spraying fallen needles into the air.

Anna stared, aghast. It wasn't a cone. It was one of her missing sandals!

Before she could think what to do, the other sandal sailed out of the branches and landed right beside the first. She jumped back, craning her head upward. And then, from the canopy of branches, came a laugh that she'd heard before, rippling like a splashing stream.

"It's you!" she exclaimed.

In response, the sand-colored bear scampered down from the boughs. With a shower of needles, he flung himself onto a branch above her head, hooked his legs over the limb, and swung upside down. He hung there, his ears dangling down and his black nose very close to her own. Close as a clam to its shell!

The bear sniffed at her face. But Anna held still. She looked straight into his eyes. How they sparkled! With wildness. And with something close to magic.

For a breathless moment, they gazed at each other. Then Anna burst into words—not really expecting the bear to understand.

"Um . . . hello. My name is Rowanna."

The bear kept peering at her, though he wrinkled his furry brow. He grunted. Then, all at once, he made a new kind of sound. *"Hashalasha nat sasharash,"* he said in a voice like swishing branches.

Anna blinked in surprise. She'd never heard words like that before. And yet somehow, in a way she could not explain, she almost understood them.

"Sasharash," she repeated. "Your name is Sasharash."

The bear pawed at her playfully. Then he swished another phrase, pointing at the rumpled bird on her shoulder.

"Oh, that's my Eagle. One day he's going to fly, but for now he keeps me company."

At this, the bear released another rippling laugh. *"Romalasha loo!"*

Eagle threw back a scornful whistle and glared at the upside-down cub.

Sasharash grasped the branch with his forepaws and swung himself upright. He shifted his four legs and stepped along the limb. Then he stopped, eyeing the beech tree across the way. His shoulders hunched. Suddenly, he leaped out of the pine and into the open air.

Anna winced, expecting him to crash to the ground. But no—he landed safely in the great beech, his paws clasping its silver branches. Leaves showered the ground as he bounced up and down. Now it was Anna's turn to laugh!

She ran to join him. "Let's climb together!"

Just as she neared the beech, though, her foot caught on a stone. She tumbled down, slamming hard into the tree trunk. Eagle shrieked and fell into a tuft of moss beside her.

Anna sat up, dazed. The bear crouched next to her. He swatted at the air and growled, *"Masha, mashamala sho?"*

"I'm all r-right," she answered weakly. "Just my leg . . ."

She halted, seeing the deep gash in her thigh. Sliced by the jagged point of a broken branch! Blood flowed, dripping down her skin and onto the moss. She'd never been cut so badly before. Never! And all that blood . . . Suddenly dizzy, she leaned back against the trunk.

Sasharash turned and bounded over to a black alder sapling at the far side of the clearing. He bit off a twig and clamped it between his paws. Then, using his teeth, he deftly stripped off the bark, like someone peeling a piece of fruit. He chewed the shredded bark for a few seconds—then raced back to the beech.

Anna, meanwhile, was trying to stop the bleeding. She pressed hard on the open wound—but nothing happened. Now blood soaked her hands as well as her leg! When the bear arrived, she looked up, her face twisted in fright.

Gently, he nudged her hands aside with his nose. He growled low, a rough sort of whisper. Then, using his tongue, he covered the gash with black alder bark.

Almost at once, the bleeding stopped. Eagle hopped nearer to her leg and chirped in surprise.

She drew a long, unsteady breath. Her body relaxed a little. She faced the bear again, this time with a quivering grin.

The cub watched her closely. And now she saw something new in his eyes, something other than wildness. Or magic. Aye, something more like friendship.

Chapter 8

ROMPING WITH A BEAR DIDN'T SEEM
odd to Anna, any more than playing with Eagle
or Old Master Burl. And with Sasharash, she
had someone just as eager as she was to climb a tree.
Or splash around in a tide pool. Or stuff herself with
fat, juicy raspberries.

The days stretched into summer and lengthened
like the golden grass at the glade. And during those
days, Anna saw plenty of her new companion. But
first, every morning, she scurried around to finish her
chores. She tended her vegetables, sharpened the old
axe, chopped some more driftwood, banked the fire
coals, and mixed some batter for kelp biscuits, turnip
cakes, or whatever she planned for that evening's
supper.

More than ever, she wanted to keep the master
content. "I must, Eagle," she'd tell the bird on
her shoulder. "So everything will go on just as
it is."

When at last her chores were done—she would join the cub and romp all afternoon. Together they climbed every tree near the cottage, waded in the shallows, stacked up huge towers of starfish, pretended they were clouds sailing high overhead, and found every last hiding place along the shore.

Once Sasharash led her to the spot where the stream gushed out of the trees and across the beach. Then, for a very long time, he sat motionless on the edge of the bank, as still as a turtle resting on a rock. Except he was no turtle, and this was no rock.

Anna got impatient. "Crab claws, Sash! What are you doing?"

The bear didn't answer. Didn't move. Not even to lick the river fly crawling on his nose.

Suddenly he sprang. His paw slapped the water and swatted a perch as big as Anna's forearm out of the stream. The fish smacked the bank, spraying water and mud all over the bear. But he only roared in glee. The perfect lunch!

Anna watched him take his first great bite. The bear tore off a piece of the tail and tossed it over to her.

"Er . . . no thanks," she said. "I like my fish cooked."

The cub wrinkled his nose in disgust, then went back to his meal.

At the end of each day, their games always stopped in time for Anna to make the master's supper. Not that Sasharash didn't growl and stomp his paws in protest! In time, though, he always let her go. She had plenty to do—including a run around the beach, to wipe away any bear prints so the old man wouldn't find them.

True enough, sometimes she had to work very fast before his boat landed. And true enough, she hardly had time now to climb Burl and wait just to catch a glimpse of the High Willow. But she didn't mind.

For now she had a friend.

Not that she dared to breathe a word to the master. Or show just how happy she felt. He would never understand! And besides, with summer's longer days, he stayed out later to fish. So while he still eyed her carefully every evening—and she wondered if he suspected something—he was too tired to say much beyond grunts and curses.

There came an afternoon when Anna and the cub rested by the glade. She chewed on a sprig of mint and leaned back against a boulder, splattered with orange lichen. "I understand your words pretty well now, Sash. Don't you think?"

The bear, lying on top of the boulder, didn't answer. He was too busy scratching his backside on the stone. He wriggled and twisted like a giant, fur-covered worm.

"Don't you?" she repeated.

The bear just wriggled some more, then reached down with one of his paws and tickled the tail feathers of the sparrow on her shoulder. Eagle shrieked and flapped his good wing.

Anna tried again. "Come now, answer me."

Finally, the cub replied. As always, he spoke in low, swishing tones. And as always, Anna understood without knowing how.

"*Mmmm*, you've learned fast enough." The bear rolled over on his chest and batted at a white moth. Then he growled, "But you should let me take you deeper into the forest! More to do there. And more to eat, too."

Anna's mint leaf lost its flavor. She spat it on the ground.

"Oh, Sash . . . You make it sound so easy."

"It is easy."

"No, it's not! I've been longing *forever* to do that.

To go right to the other side of the forest and up the ridge. All the way to the High Willow." She sighed. "Did I tell you the master found me there?"

The cub made a growl that was closer to a groan. "Three times already."

"Right there among the roots," she went on dreamily. "And someday . . . well, someday I'm going back. Sure as sea foam, I am!" Her chest heaved in a sigh. "It's what I want most, Sash. More than anything."

The bear just shrugged. "Why do you care so much where you came from? It's just a place."

"Oh, no! It's much more than that. It's *my* place— my beginning. Seeing it will help me see myself. Who I really am."

He snorted. "You don't know that already?"

"No." Her eyes clouded. "I don't."

With his tongue, he licked the very tip of his nose. "Whatever you think about that place, it doesn't matter. You'll never go back there."

Anna sat up—so sharply that the sparrow nearly tumbled off her shoulder. "What do you mean by that?"

Sash stretched out his paw to a gorseberry bush beside the boulder. He growled in concentration, aimed carefully, then swatted one plump berry clean off its stem. The berry sailed high in the air. Meanwhile, the cub swung himself around and opened his jaws—just in time to catch the flying treat on his tongue. He swallowed and smacked his lips.

"Tell me," said Anna with a growl of her own.

"Tell you what?"

"Rotting ravens, Sash! Why you said I'm not going!"

The cub eyed her darkly. "If you won't let me take you any deeper in the forest, how can you ever get to the High Willow?"

She frowned. "I don't know." She lowered her voice, unsure who might be listening in the trees beyond the glade. Even the old beech, friendly as it seemed on the surface, might be hiding something else.

"It's . . . the ghouls. I'm not ready to face them."

"Why are you whispering?"

She just bit her lip.

Sash thumped her shoulder with his paw. "Anna, listen to me! *There are no forest ghouls.*"

She scoffed. "You're joking."

"Me? Joke?" The bear turned his attention to trying to curl his tongue all the way around his longest claw. Suddenly he poked himself, yelped, and shook his tongue hard for several seconds. Then he turned back to Anna. "I never joke."

She smirked at him.

"Not about that, anyway." He growled deeply. "No ghouls here. Just trees and whatever creatures live in them."

"But I've heard stories! Lots of them."

Sash gave a snort, more like a wild boar than a cub. "From who? Master Meanface himself?"

"Now, now." Anna's brow furrowed. "He can be a sour old turnip, I grant you that. But he wouldn't lie."

"Well then, he's got barnacles for brains. And so do you if you listen to him." He sat up on the boulder, his fur rippling in the sun's rays. "Here, I'll prove it to you."

Shoulders tense and eyes alert, he scanned the surrounding trees. Suddenly he spotted the upright trunk of a tree killed by lightning, and grunted gladly.

Anna shook her head. Surely he wasn't going to climb that old thing! Its slippery smooth trunk, with no bark or branches, would be impossible. And besides, what did that have to do with the ghouls?

All at once, the bear leaped off the boulder. He wrapped his legs around the charred trunk and began to work his way upward. As he gouged the claws of his forepaws into the wood, his hind legs groped for a knot to hold his weight. Bit by bit, he edged higher.

"Thundering thumbnails, Sash! What are you doing?"

He just kept climbing. When he reached halfway, more than twice Anna's height off the ground, he came to a stubby bit of branch. But as soon as he grasped it with his paw, the stub broke off. Sash lost his grip and slid most of the way back down, his claws scraping the trunk.

With a fierce growl, he started up again. Faster than before! By the time he passed the broken stub, chips of wood dotted his snout and clung to his ears. The muscles of his shoulders shook from the strain.

Anna watched, her heart thumping along with his. Somehow, beneath his furry coating, he seemed not so much a bear as a person just like herself. Almost . . . a boy. *Whatever you're doing, Sash—don't fall. Please don't fall.*

Higher he climbed, and higher. Now he was nearly four times as tall as Anna. She glimpsed some berries at the top of the trunk: a wreath of llyrberries, ripe and round. Was that what this was all about?

Now the top was almost in reach. With one last

heave, his paw caught the rim. The trunk must have been hollow, since he reached right down inside. At last, he hauled himself up to the top, straightened his back, and roared in triumph.

Sure enough, Sash grabbed a great pawful of berries and crammed them into his mouth. Yellow juice dribbled down his furry neck. Then he stood up on his hind legs, balanced on the rim.

"Careful now," Anna called up to him. "You'd squash like one of those berries if you fell."

The cub ignored her and started to jump on the rim. "Look here, all you ghouls!" he cried. "Come and get me if you can!"

Anna sucked in her breath. Anxiously, she looked into the dark mass of branches beyond the glade. "Don't be foolish, Sash."

The bear didn't seem to hear. "Watch this, you stupid ghouls! My newest dance step."

He kicked one leg outward, balancing on just one paw. Anna chewed her lip as she watched. The next instant he leaped into the air and did a full turn. His body spun around in a sand-colored blur. With a wild cry, he landed safely again on the rim.

All of a sudden, a chunk of wood beneath him broke off. Sash's cry rose to a shriek. His claws raked the air as he toppled backward—right into the hollow trunk!

There came another cry, this one muffled, and a powerful thud that rocked the whole tree. Then silence.

Chapter 9

ANNA JUMPED TO HER FEET. SHE raced over to the trunk where the cub had disappeared. Wind gusted through the surrounding trees, making them shudder and spray leaves and cones across the ground. A gorseberry bush rattled like a pod of seeds in a storm.

"Sash!" She beat her fists against the trunk's lightning-charred wood. "Are you hurt?"

No answer.

"Sash! Can you hear me?"

Still no answer.

Anna turned to the dark forest beyond the glade. Were ghouls out there, just hidden from sight? Had they done this to Sash?

She wiped her brow with her forearm and turned back to the tree. Setting her ear against a knothole in the trunk, she listened. Eagle paced to and fro on her shoulder. Then, from inside the tree, she heard a muffled groan.

"Sash!" she shouted straight into the knothole. "Talk to me!"

"Some . . . dance step," came the weak reply. "Guess I need . . . more practice."

"Forget that, you crazy bear! Can you climb out?"

"N-no. Can't . . . climb." He groaned as he shifted himself. "These walls—too slippery. *Aaagh*. And my leg . . ."

She braced her feet in the tangle of roots and pushed hard against the trunk. Her shoulder flattened, and her legs shook with strain. She knew she couldn't push over such a big tree. But mayhaps she could tilt it some—enough that he could crawl out.

With all her strength, she heaved. But the tree just wouldn't budge.

"Ohhh," moaned the muffled voice. "It hurts, Anna. Hurts bad."

"What, your leg?"

"No, my belly! I'm hungrier . . . by the second. Can't you at least . . . throw me some berries?"

She knew he was trying to make her laugh. But she could also hear the raw pain in his voice. "Forget about your belly for once!" She glared at the knothole. "I'll find some way to get you out, I promise."

She licked her dry lips. But how? She couldn't

climb up the trunk herself. Besides, even if she could, what good would it do? And what about the ghouls?

Casting her eyes around the glade, she searched for something—anything—she could use. No luck! All she saw were leaves, branches, and shafts of fern. Then she spotted a thin purple vine curled around the limb of a sapling. An idea burst into her mind like a dolphin leaping into the air. Mayhaps . . . If she could just drop down a vine—one long enough to reach— he might be able to climb out.

Where, though, to find a vine that big? And sturdy? She slapped her forehead. The vines the master used for his nets!

From inside the trunk, her friend groaned again. Louder this time.

"I'll be back, Sash," she called. "Very soon." She set down Eagle on the roots. "Stay here, now. Keep him company."

She dashed back to the cottage, crashing through the bramble bushes that lined the shore. Breathing hard, she scanned the remains of the old nets that lay on the beach. But they were just tangled bits of vines. She needed one as long as a rope. Aye, like the ones the master—

She stiffened. *Like the ones he gathered from the*

forest. She knew, from what he'd said, that he fetched them somewhere up the stream where Sash had caught the perch. How far upstream he went, she didn't know—just that he followed the rill into the woods.

Deep into the woods.

She sucked in her breath. Ghouls or no ghouls, she would go!

Anna started running down the shore, to the deep-rutted spot where the stream emptied into the sea. At the edge of the bank, she turned into the forest. She ran beside the stream, her feet slapping on the mud, even as sharp branches tore at her arms and legs.

The forest grew steadily darker. And denser. Trees crowded closer to the bank—aye, with roots that gouged the ground like claws. Branches dripped with spray. Moss hung everywhere, wet and thick. So thick that sometimes she had to wade into the stream itself to get by. And crab claws, it was cold! Icy water slapped her legs and tried to knock her down. Once her foot slipped on an underwater rock and she almost fell into the dark, dripping arms of the trees.

A sound! She stopped to listen as water swirled around her feet. High and wailing it came, thinner than a spider's thread.

The sound grew louder, nearer, rising with the wind. Then more sounds joined in—shrieks, howls, and moans. Did all that come from the wind in the trees? Or from something else?

Anna shuddered and kept walking up the stream. Her toes felt numb from cold. But step by step, she pushed deeper into the forest.

At last she reached a bend where the bank lifted into a sheer wall of rock. Tiny rills poured down the cliff and splattered into the stream. Vines—long, twisted ones—grew there by the dozens, hanging like loose green hairs. This was what she'd been looking for.

She hesitated. What if the ghouls tried to stop her? Had they ever attacked the master when he'd come here for vines? She wished now that she'd thought to bring along his axe.

Cautiously, she waded over to the base of the cliff. Then she reached for one of the longest vines, wrapped it around her wrist—and tugged. It held fast, like an oyster to its rock.

"Come on, now!" she commanded. "I need you. Sash needs you!"

She dug her feet into the stony stream bottom,

leaned back, and tugged again. All at once the vine pulled loose. She fell back in the stream with a splash.

Water gushed from her leggings as she stood. She gathered up the vine, coiled it into loops, and turned to go. Just then a new wind, fiercer than before, swept through the forest. Branches creaked and groaned, and trees swayed all around. A hefty branch broke off and crashed in the water right beside her.

Suddenly she glimpsed a shape—not quite a face. As twisted as a knot of roots. Watching her from behind an oak!

Anna gasped. The face peered at her with ghoulish, night-dark eyes. Then what looked like a ragged, toothy mouth started to open . . .

She ran, faster than she'd ever run before, back down the stream, to the beach, and finally to the glade. When at last she reached the trunk, she staggered over, panting hoarsely. Eagle chirped a loud welcome. She dropped the vine and put her mouth to the knothole.

"I'm back, Sash."

A low moan came from inside the trunk.

She almost told him what she'd seen—then stopped herself. That could wait.

Anna grabbed the vine and tied a stone to one end.

Planting her feet, she started to hurl it up to the rim. Suddenly, she froze. The vine wasn't big enough! Long as it was, it wouldn't reach all the way down the trunk to Sash.

She spun to face the lichen-covered boulder where they had sat only moments before. That just might do it!

Hastily she scaled the boulder. She tied the free end of the vine around her waist. Then she hefted the weighted end in her hand, judging her aim. At last she threw the vine at the top of the trunk. It missed— glancing off the side with a spray of wood chips.

She gathered up the vine and threw again. This time, the stone at the end struck the rim and knocked off some yellow berries. But the vine's weight pulled it back down. With a slap, it hit the ground.

"Rotting ravens!" She stamped her foot on the boulder. Taking the vine once more, she drew a deep breath, reared back—and threw. She watched as it flew upward, hit the rim, and like a slithering snake, plunged down the hole. She'd done it!

"Grab hold!" she shouted. "And climb!"

Nothing happened.

She shook the bottom of the vine. "Grab it!"

Seconds passed. And more seconds.

All at once the vine jerked. Then went taut. Then jerked again, and again. He was climbing!

Anna grabbed hold and pulled down with her own weight. *Don't break, vine—please don't break.*

Finally, she spotted a slight movement at the rim. Sash! Something emerged from the hollow trunk and grabbed the edge. But to Anna's shock, it wasn't his paw. Or anyone's paw.

It was a hand.

Chapter 10

AN INSTANT LATER, THE HAND that had grasped the rim of the trunk melted back into a bear paw. Right before her eyes! Anna, watching from the boulder, blinked in surprise. She looked overhead at the shimmering rays that sliced through the branches, then back at the paw.

Again she blinked. *Must have been just a trick of light.*

After the paw, a shaggy bear emerged from the hollow trunk. Sash was covered with spiderwebs, dust, and wood chips. And when he pulled out his left rear paw, it looked twisted and swollen. But he was alive! Anna laughed out loud when he thrust his snout into the yellow llyrberries at the rim of the trunk and took a huge bite.

The cub swallowed the berries at once. Streams of juice rolled down the sides of his mouth. He waved at Anna, then rested on the rim, breathing hard.

Finally, he wriggled backward and wrapped his

hind legs around the top of the trunk. Then, despite his swollen paw, he slid back down the outside of the tree. His claws squealed as they scraped against the wood. With a thump, he landed on the ground.

Anna jumped off the boulder and stepped over to his side. He brushed some bark off his furry chest and gazed up at her, green eyes aglow.

"Thanks, Anna."

"Oh," she replied casually, "I'd do that for any old bear. Even one crazy enough to dare the ghouls."

He laughed, the same rippling laugh she had heard so many times before. But this time it sounded a bit different—lighter, somehow, and the voice a little higher. His laughter lifted into the surrounding trees, whose branches rustled and creaked along with him.

"How's this feeling?" She gently pulled a spider-web off the hurt limb.

The cub straightened his leg and let the paw sink into a thick tuft of moss. "Just needs some rest, that's all."

"Which won't be easy for you."

Eagle hopped closer on a root and chirped in agreement.

The young bear pushed his nose at Anna. "No, but

I can take care of myself. Always have." He cocked his head. "Until . . . just now."

He reached his forepaw toward her face. Lightly he touched her cheek, so lightly that he seemed to have no claws at all. "You're the crazy one, you know," he said, his voice sounding higher again. "But that's the way I like . . . a friend."

Puddles formed in Anna's eyes. For a moment, in her clouded vision, he looked less like a bear than a sandy-haired boy. A boy who had called her *friend*.

She reached up to touch the paw on her cheek. What she felt, though, was not a paw—but a hand. A hand with fingers like her own.

She shrieked and pulled away. Furiously, she blinked, trying to clear her vision. Nothing changed. The bear cub before her was now, indeed, a boy.

He wore little over his walnut brown skin: loose leggings made of woven strips of bark, and a band of scarlet leaves around one wrist. His bare chest and arms bore dozens of scrapes, bruises, and scars. Gone was all the fur, though his sandy hair looked just as unruly. Only his wild, magical eyes, as green as the forest itself, hadn't changed.

The boy watched her, a mysterious gleam in those eyes. "So what do you see?"

"A boy! You're a boy!" She shook her head in disbelief. "How . . . ?"

"I'm still Sash," he said calmly.

Anna couldn't stop shaking her head. "But who *are* you, really?"

With his good wing, Eagle tapped the boy's knee, as if demanding an answer.

Sash's gaze never wavered. "Guess."

"Just tell me!"

"No, guess." He grinned with all the mischief of a cub—but the face of a boy.

She drew a deep breath. "Well . . . you're *not* a bear."

He nodded. "Right so far." He picked up a llyrberry that had dropped into the grass, flicked it into the air, and caught it on his tongue. "Though I like the way they eat."

"And eat and eat."

"Right again." He folded his arms on his chest. "Come on, now. I thought you had a brain! Can't you do any better?"

She growled at him, sounding like a bear herself. "Well, I just don't know. You're not a bear, and you're not a regular boy. Aye, that's certain! What *are* you, then?"

He just kept grinning.

Anna's brow furrowed. "Oh, come on. Give me a hint, at least."

Sash pursed his lips. "All right, all right. I guess you could say I'm, well . . . closer to Old Burl."

"Old Burl?" She stared at him, now thoroughly confused. "He's back at the beach! And we're out here, by the glade. You're no closer than I am, and you know it."

"Not like that, Anna." His eyes sparkled. "Closer *in spirit*."

She gasped. And her mouth opened as wide as an oyster. "You don't mean . . . you're not saying . . ."

He leaned nearer. "What?"

She blew a long, slow breath. "You're not really . . ."

"I am! A tree spirit."

She just stood there, dumbfounded.

"What my people call a *drumalo*." He bent his injured leg, winced, then put it back down on the moss. "And what some might call a tree ghoul."

Anna felt suddenly wobbly. She sat down, her back against the trunk of the hollow tree. And gazed at him with round eyes. "But . . . ," she said at last, "tree ghouls are horrid, and ugly." She glanced over her shoulder. "I saw one, Sash. Deep in the forest. It had the scariest face."

Sash reached his hands up to his face and pulled at the sides of his mouth. He crossed his eyes and wagged his tongue. And he started making strange noises—a mix of snarls, snorts, and hiccups.

"Like that?" he asked.

She shook her head. "Be serious. The ghouls are deadly!"

"How many times do I have to tell you? There are no ghouls. Just drumalos, like me."

She gazed at him, her hazel eyes full of doubt.

Sash laid his hand on her knee. "You can be pretty thick, you know. I've met moles who are smarter."

"Say now, that's not fair! I learned your language, didn't I? Fast as . . . well, fast as a seal can sail on the waves."

"*Ha!* You mean fast as an owl can sail on the wind."

She nodded, her face suddenly serious. "If what you say is true . . ."

"Anna, believe me. It's true."

She studied him for a long moment. "Now I know why your words sound so much like branches swishing."

He peered back at her. "And there's more for you to know. Aye, much more."

"Wait now! What I really want to know is why you're *not* scary. Like you're supposed to be."

He smirked. "I'm scary to my mother sometimes."

"No, no. I'm not joking! Aren't tree spirits really . . . well, *ghouls*?"

Sash straightened his back against the trunk. "Only if that's what you're expecting."

"You mean . . ."

"Aye! Don't you see, Anna? That's a drumalo's special skill. We look like whatever you most expect, or want, to see. A bear cub—or a boy."

"Or a ghoul!" She pursed her lips, trying to take all this in. "You can really do that?"

"Right."

A fresh wind swept through the forest, tossing branches all around. Leaves and twigs and petals swirled through the honey-sweet air. For a while they just listened to the swish of boughs and the rustle of grass.

Sash reached over and took her hand. "It's for our own protection. This way, to a bear cub—or someone watching bear cubs—that's what I look like. And if you're expecting an ugly old ghoul, well, that's what you'll find."

Her heart raced just at the thought of the hideous face she'd seen in the forest. "This is all so hard to believe."

"Of course, we only take those shapes," he went on, "when we're uprooting."

"Uprooting?"

"Traveling around, outside our home trees." He flexed his leg on the bed of moss. "Me, I was born in a grove of hawthorns. At the far end of the forest, near that old willow you've talked about."

Anna started. Her eyes glowed like newborn stars. "The High Willow? You've been there?"

"Grew up dancing around her roots! Aye, and swinging from her branches." He chuckled to himself. "Riding out storms there, too. Big, howling ones! Enough to blow me and my whole family to the ocean and back."

She smiled. "And you have lots of family, I'll wager. Five or six hawthorn brothers and sisters?"

"Five or six!" he bellowed. "Why, I've got thousands! When you're a drumalo, the whole *forest* is your family."

Anna drew a deep breath. Being a tree spirit sounded so very different from what she'd expected. From what she'd been taught. Amazing! Mayhaps the master was just mistaken? But was that really possible?

She slid closer on the gnarled roots. "Sash, you have to tell me the truth about something."

"Me? I always tell the truth, you know that."

"Really, now." She bowed her head toward his so their noses almost touched. "Do tree ghouls—spirits, I mean—ever harm people? Or kill them?"

He scrunched up his nose, as if she'd asked him to bite himself. "Is that what old Crabface told you?"

"Aye. But it's not true, is it?"

He made his mock scary face again, complete with snorts and hiccups. "What do you think, Anna?"

"I'd say it's not what drumalos do."

"And you'd be right."

She slapped her own thigh. "So they couldn't have killed her!"

"Who?"

"My mother!" Her voice rose, even as the surrounding branches chattered and swished. "The tree ghouls didn't kill her! Oh, Sash, I've got to find out what really happened to her. Got to! She could still be alive, you know." She swallowed. "And even if she's not . . . then at least I'll know."

She squeezed his arm. "Take me there, would you?

To the High Willow? Right to the place I was found! Please, Sash? Please?"

Somberly, he shook his head. "Sorry. I just can't."

Anna just looked at him. A bumblebee hummed right past her cheek, but she didn't notice. "Can't?"

He shook his head again.

Tears welled in her eyes, though she tried to blink them back.

"Until my ankle heals, that is!" He laughed, his voice rippling like a swollen stream. "When I'm better, I'll come for you. And take you there."

She hooted with delight and hugged him.

Suddenly Eagle started to whistle. Anna looked up at the slanting rays of sunlight, woven through the branches like gleaming threads of gold. Late afternoon already!

"Oh!" she cried. "The master—he'll be back soon." She lifted the sparrow onto her shoulder. "I've got to go. But will you be all right?"

"Sure," he replied, with a broad sweep of his arm. "I've got plenty of family to look after me."

Chapter 11

DAYS WENT BY, DAYS THAT FELT LIKE weeks to Anna. The air hummed with insects and rustling leaves, and sunlight warmed the sand late into the evening. Summer had truly begun.

These were the days Anna usually loved most. But now she barely noticed. For her mind was filled, like the shallows at high tide, with questions about Sash. When would he come for her? And would he still want to take her to the willow?

As she stepped along the water's edge one late afternoon, the cool waves licked her feet. Wet sand slid between her toes. And she wondered about her coming journey with Sash. Would it really be as safe as he thought? What if all tree spirits weren't as kind and playful as he was? Mayhaps some of them really *were* ghouls.

She shuddered, remembering that face in the forest. And all the master's gruesome tales of poor creatures killed by ghouls—creatures whose eyes had been ripped out of their skulls, whose skin had been torn to bits by cruel claws, and whose bloody innards had been draped from trees.

Seeing Old Burl, she strode over and sat on one of the fir's knobby roots. That familiar smell, both tart and sweet, rolled over her like a wave. And calmed her, as it always did. As she sat there in the cool shade, Eagle, who had been busy pecking clamshells on the beach, hopped to her side.

Anna gazed up into the layers of needled branches. "What should I believe, Burl? Is Sash really a tree spirit?" She tilted her head slightly. "Are you?"

The tree gave a quiet creak of its trunk. No more.

She closed her eyes and rested her head against Old Burl's trunk. She could almost feel something in there. Something that stirred with a life of its own. Was it a spirit? Or just a bark beetle? She couldn't be sure.

Her eyes opened and turned to the forest—and what lay beyond. The far ridge was covered with mist, like a blanket that someone had woven from wisps of cloud. What was it, really, that drew her to the High Willow? The memory of her mother, or something else?

She shook her head. She couldn't be sure of that, either. Mayhaps she wasn't really remembering her mother, but only those songs she would sing. Songs that blew like the wind . . . and beat like a heart.

That evening, after a supper of crabmeat cakes and mackerel soup, the master checked carefully all the door and window latches. "Can't be too blasted careful," he grumbled. "'Tis a full moon tonight, and them ghouls will be out a-prowlin'."

He swung his face toward her. The orange glow from the hearth flickered on his brow, as if his thoughts were on fire. "Ye haven't seen any more bears recently, have ye, girl?"

Anna looked up from the leggings she was trying to repair. "No," she answered truthfully. But she frowned, wishing she could open her whole heart to him. The way she could long ago, when she was little.

"Good." The old man reached for his pipe, stuffed some dried kelp in the bowl—then cast it aside. "Aaah! I be too thunderin' tired for even a smoke. These summer days be long ones, and brutal."

Anna felt a surge of sympathy. "You've done well, sir, with your catches."

"Well enough," he replied, his voice a touch softer. "Got to keep us fed, I do." His gray eyes glowed like coals in the firelight. He looked at her almost warmly.

"Yer gettin' bigger, girl. And I wants ye to keep on growin'."

She grinned at the corners of her mouth. "That's why I need to lengthen these leggings."

"And why ye needs yer sleep." She wasn't sure, but he almost seemed to grin himself. "Get now, to bed with ye."

Moments later, Anna lay on her pallet of straw. She watched the firelight flicker on the thatch above, and felt warmed by something more than the hearth. And she knew she would sleep well tonight.

But she was wrong. She rolled and turned. Bits of straw poked at her neck. And someone was calling to her, calling her name.

"Anna," the voice called. "Rowanna."

She sat up. Fingers of moonlight were reaching through the cracks in the shutter, groping at the edge of her pallet. She listened, trying to hear the voice that had called to her. All she heard, though, was the splash of surf outside the cottage.

Yet someone had truly called. She was sure of it. Sash? No . . . not him, but someone else. Aye, someone she knew. But who? And she could still hear that voice now—not with her ears, but deeper, in her bones.

Outside. Right now, waiting for me. She stood up and walked across the earthen floor. *The master— mustn't wake him. He needs to sleep.*

Almost in a dream, she tiptoed past the master, sound asleep. Ever so quietly, she glided to the door. When her hand touched the latch, though, she froze. Should she really do this? Was there something wrong with opening the door, something she couldn't remember?

But the pull to go outside was too strong. She slid open the latch. Cold night air slapped her face and flowed right through her grass nightshirt. She shivered, then stepped onto the beach.

Old Burl stood motionless, watching. The fir's branches glittered in the silvery light. And behind, a great globe was rising over the forest, glowing brighter by the second. The rising moon!

Had the moon somehow called to her? She watched, entranced, as it lifted over the trees and into the sky as dark as octopus ink. Its light made a pathway across the clouds. A pathway that shone like the sunlit sea.

Suddenly she caught her breath. For the shining path led across the sky and straight to the highest knoll on the ridge. And ended at the single tree that stood there, all alone. Aye, the High Willow had

never looked so clear as it did tonight! Its arching
branches seemed to glow with a light of their own.

Anna knew, in a flash, who had called her name.
The willow! She stepped closer to the forest edge. *I
will come to you, I will. And I promise—*

"Thunder and blast, girl! What be ye doin' out here
at night?"

The master stood at the cottage door. He glared at
her, the moonlight in his eyes as bright as lightning
bolts. Then, as he saw where she was looking, he
strode over and seized her by the shoulders.

"I should've known, ye brainless child! Lookin'
right into the eyes of that ghoul on the ridge!"

"B-but sir . . . ," she sputtered. "It's n-not like
that."

"What?" He squeezed her shoulders. "Are ye
sayin' there be no ghoul there?"

"*Oww*," she squealed, trying to pull away. "I'm
saying mayhaps there's more to that tree than we
know."

He squeezed her harder.

"*Ow*, Master, please! You're hurting me."

His face twisted and he relaxed his grip a little.
"That tree be terrible dangerous, girl. Terrible dangerous! Surely ye know that by now."

She shook her head, as mist filled her eyes.

For a long moment he peered down at her. His own eyes grew clouded. "I jest don't want to lose ye, child. Not after everythin' I—"

He caught himself. His tongue worked inside his mouth, as if he wanted to swallow some words he just could not speak. Finally, in a raspy voice, he commanded, "Now go. Back inside where ye belong! Afore them ghouls be comin' for ye."

As the door slammed behind them, a new breeze arose, leaning on Old Master Burl. The tree's moonlit branches sagged lower, and made a sound very much like a sigh.

Chapter 12

AS THE DAYS GREW LONGER, ANNA'S hunger to go to the willow grew sharper. Not even the warm waves that sloshed upon the shore, or the seal pups who played on the sand, could distract her now.

"Is this the day? Will Sash come this morning?" She woke up every day with the same questions on her mind.

Meanwhile, she hardly even spoke with the master. His face looked hard these days. Aye, and brittle as dried thatch.

One morning, just after the master had dragged his boat into the surf and rowed off for the day, Anna sat down beside Old Burl. She put her hand on a mound of needles between two roots—and felt something move. What was this? Looking closer, she saw a tiny pink paw. She pushed aside the needles.

A nest of mice! The mother mouse lay on her side,

while four babies as pink as rosebuds squirmed beneath her, trying to suckle. A fifth one had rolled away, and squeaked for help. Anna nudged the little mouse back to where it belonged, while the mother watched with bright black eyes.

Anna covered them again with needles. Then she scanned the forest edge. Still no Sash! She slapped the side of the tree and demanded, "Where is that bear? Why hasn't he come?"

The old tree stirred ever so slightly. A single fleck of bark fell to the ground, spinning all the way.

"I've got to go back there, Burl. If I don't, I'll just die!" She drew a long breath. "Oh, Burl! What if Sash isn't coming at all?"

Needles rustled in the fir's upper boughs.

"I *am* being patient. I am, I tell you!"

But still Sash didn't come.

More days passed. Anna watched and waited for some sign from him. Yet none came.

Then, at last, the sign appeared. Or more truly, it disappeared. For one day, when she was outside pulling radishes, her sandals vanished. One minute she set them down by the garden's edge—and the next minute, they were gone.

It had to be him! She scooped up Eagle and put him

in her apron pocket. Then she dashed through the brambles and into the forest.

Near the glade, she stopped. There were her sandals—hanging from a branch of the great beech. And there, hanging beside them in the silvery boughs, was her friend. The upside-down boy waved both his hands. His dangling hair seemed to shoot straight out of his head.

Anna grabbed a low branch, swung her leg over, and scampered up the tree as fast as a squirrel. When she reached Sash, she slid over to the spot where his legs wrapped around the branch. And started tickling the bottoms of his feet.

"*Hoohoo,* now stop that! *Hoohoohoo heehee ho-ho-ho.* Anna, stop!" He turned himself over and sat upright beside her. His whole face scowled. "That was mean."

"So was making me wait so long!"

His green eyes glittered. "Missed me, didn't you?"

"*Mmm,* not really." She almost smiled. "Eagle and I, we've been dancing day and night."

"Oh, I'm sure."

Anna tapped her toes against the smooth bark of the beech. "When can we go, Sash?"

He looked puzzled. "Go where?"

"The High Willow! Like you promised."

"Did I?" He rubbed his chin slowly. "I *never* make promises."

"Oh, you! Stop the joking, all right?" She frowned at him. "Really, sometimes I think I liked you better as a bear!"

"If that's what you want to see, I can always change back."

"What I want is to go to the willow!"

"Really, now? Why didn't you say so?" He broke off a twig and tossed it at her. "So when do you want to go?"

"Now!" She nodded several times. "Right now."

"Fine. Old Fungusface will just have to make his own supper tonight."

Anna, who had already started climbing down the beech, suddenly froze. "You mean we can't do it in a day?"

He smirked. "Not unless you can fly."

Cheeeyup! The sparrow in her apron pocket started squawking loudly.

"Right, Eagle. You're right." Anna reached down and stroked his rumpled feathers. "You're the only one of us who'll ever fly." Then she turned back to Sash. "How long is the trek?"

"Two days, at least."

"Two days!" Her face fell. "But . . ."

"Oh, come on, now. Let the old man make his own biscuits for once."

"It's not that, Sash."

"So what's wrong, then?"

"It's . . . well, there's no telling *what* he might do if he finds me gone! And when I come back, he—" She shook her head. "No, no, I don't even want to think about that."

She hit the beech's trunk with her fist. "Wait! I have an idea!" Quickly, she climbed back up and sat on the branch beside him. "In just about a week, he goes out to the Farthest Reef to fish. It's a long trip, and he needs lots of daylight to do it. So he goes only once a year. On the longest day of summer."

"High Hallow Eve," said the boy quietly. "He leaves you alone on *that* night?"

Anna gave a slow nod. Below, in the ferns at the edge of the glade, she saw a young hedgehog nuzzling its mother's side. "Aye, and that's when we'll make our own journey."

A mysterious smile lit Sash's face. "That's a special night in the forest, too, you know."

"What do you mean, special?"

His eyes flashed strangely. "You'll see. Soon enough."

Chapter 13

A T LAST, THE DAY ARRIVED. AYE, and none too soon!

Anna could hardly contain herself as she helped Master Mellwyn get ready for his trip to the Farthest Reef. She wrapped some scallop cakes, mended his shroud, and checked all his nets—all the while trying to keep her excitement from showing. So she spun no twirls and sang no songs.

But crab claws, it was hard!

After breakfast, the master sat in the driftwood chair by the hearth, chewing on the stem of his pipe. He blew a puff of greenish smoke. And watched Anna closely.

"The moon will be out tonight, girl. And almost full."

She looked up from the flask she'd been filling with water. "Aye, sir."

"And ye recall what happened afore, that dreadful night?"

"Aye, sir."

He puffed some more, eyeing her all the while. "Ye promise not to forget what I told ye?"

Anna swallowed and tried to keep her voice steady. "I promise."

He continued to watch her pour the water. "Mayhaps I shouldn't go at all this year."

Her hands squeezed the flask, but she said nothing. She just returned his gaze in silence. But under her apron, her heart was pounding like the surf in a summer squall.

In time, he spoke again. "Blast that larder of ours! Hard as I've worked, it still be almost empty. And we'll be needin' some bigger fish for smokin', if we're not to starve this winter." He tapped his pipe against the palm of his hand. "So I guess I must be goin' after all."

Anna barely nodded.

An hour later, the master shoved off. As he rowed across the lagoon, morning light gleamed on the waves like a web of spun gold. Anna watched from the window as his boat, loaded down with extra nets, lines, and bait, vanished over the horizon. Then she grabbed her own supplies—a shredded cloak and a pocketful of radishes—and scurried out the door.

She paused just long enough to step over to Old

Burl, who stood as always by the cottage. She drank in the smell one more time, and patted the fir's rough bark. Then, without looking back, she plunged into the woods.

Sash met her at the glade. The boy reached up to tickle Eagle, who was riding on her shoulder—and got nipped in return. With a laugh, he started off, Anna at his side. They walked fast, bare feet slapping on the leaves and lichens. Not fast enough, though! Anna broke into a run, jumping over the rocks and broken branches on the ground. Sash padded along beside her.

Soon I'll be there, she said to herself. She might even learn, before this day was out, what really happened at the High Willow. To herself. And to her mother—whose face she couldn't remember, but whose songs still held her heart.

The sun's rays poked through the trees, wavering like branches of light. Anna and Sash ran across parades of toadstools and beds of blue-green moss. And oh, the aromas! She smelled the mustiness of wood turning to soil, the sweetness of resins warmed by the sun, the tanginess of rillberries washed by a stream. And more, too—so many smells, she couldn't even start to name them all.

"Slow down, Anna." Sash, running by her side, tapped her shoulder. "You'll be all tired out before we're halfway to the ridge."

Anna just shook her head. Her steps were getting more choppy, but she tried to run even faster. "We've got to make it," she panted, "all the way . . . there and back . . . by tomorrow night."

"We'll make it."

"But not if—" She tried to leap over a broken branch, but caught her foot and crashed to the ground. She rolled into some ferns.

Sash bent over her. He pushed aside the ferns, not bothering to hide his smirk. "Ready to walk now?"

"No, you old barnacle!" She stood and pulled some leaves out of her hair. And then pulled Eagle out of the tangle of brush where he'd landed. "But I will, I guess." She elbowed Sash. "So long as you're sure we can make it."

"I'm sure. That is, if you'll quit taking naps in the ferns."

They set off again. Into the trees they plunged— trees with more shapes and sizes and colors than Anna had ever dreamed possible. So many different kinds! Even their shadows were different: tall and poky for pines, soft and round for rowans, dark and patchy for hawthorns.

How could she have ever thought of the forest as a single thing? It seemed that way from the shore, all right. But no, it was really more like a village—a village of trees. And everyone who lived there was as different from the others as Old Burl was from the silver beech at the glade.

There stood an ash tree, holding a family of raccoons with star-bright eyes. And there—a young elm, swaying gracefully as they strode past. It didn't just carry its leaves, but wore them, as a dancer would wear a shimmering gown. Beyond stood a spruce tree, its trunk stooped and bent, its branches sweeping the ground. And over there, an ancient oak, spreading great arms over the saplings that grew at its roots.

What path they followed, Anna couldn't tell. If there was a path at all! Sash seemed to see one, though. Or at least to sense where they were going.

In time, Anna started to notice other things. Branches, on every side, that snapped and creaked and groaned. Leaves that rustled like someone's raspy breath. And cries, strange and haunting, that echoed through the trees.

Hard as she tried, she couldn't forget the master's stories. Couldn't stop wondering what the spirits of all these trees were doing. Aye, right now!

They passed through a thick grove of evergreens. Suddenly she caught sight of something moving beside them. A shadow! One that looked like a tree—but strode with long, floppy steps. She whirled around and peered into the dark mass of trunks, roots, and branches.

Nothing.

She rubbed her chin. Where had that shadow gone? This was all too strange. And strangest of all . . . the shadow reminded her somehow of Old Burl.

"Come on!" Sash waved at her from up ahead. He was standing by a sunlit walnut tree, whose branches smelled like nuts roasting on a hearth. "We've got a long way to go."

She ran to him. Right away, they set off again. And they continued, never slowing, across ground muddy and dry, steep and flat, sunlit and shadowed.

Before long, Anna noticed something new. As the day went on, the trees grew quieter. Much quieter. A hush came over the forest, filling it like a mist.

Fewer branches clacked or groaned, fewer leaves whispered. Even the squirrels stopped their chatter.

Before long, there was almost no sound at all, but for two pairs of padding feet.

Rotting ravens, she thought. *What's going on?*

At last they paused for a drink at a rushing rill. Anna cupped her hands and filled them, while Eagle hopped over to the edge of the bank. For his part, Sash plunged his whole head into the water. Then he shook himself, splattering the others. Eagle squawked and slapped the air with his good wing.

Anna leaned back against a young beech, whose smooth bark shone like a sea-washed shell. "Sash, why does it feel like the trees are, well . . . *waiting* for something?"

"You feel it?" He gave a small grin, but said no more.

Onward they trekked, over a hill blackened by fire years before, and around the edge of a mist-shrouded marsh. For lunch, they ate the tops of some stalks of golden grass that Sash called *nutashala,* along with some of Anna's radishes. Then they continued on their way, rounding a lake nearly covered with lily pads. Fat green frogs sat on the leaves, strangely silent.

All the while, the quiet grew heavier. Like a storm cloud ready to burst.

As the late afternoon light shafted through the branches, the land started to rise steadily. Up they climbed, over rocks and tumbled trunks, as if they were mounting a stairway to the sky. Anna's thighs stiffened, and her calves ached. But even more, she felt the weight of all that stillness. That growing tension in the air.

And she felt something more—a subtle thrill swelling in her chest. For she knew, without asking, that they had started to climb the great ridge. Not far now! She craned her neck and peered up into the mesh of boughs. She couldn't see the top of the ridge, or the willow that stood there. Not yet, anyway.

But she was close. Really close.

The slope grew steeper. Her knees and calves throbbed. She knew that she'd need to rest sometime soon. But how could she stop now?

Just then Sash pointed to a carpet of thick moss under a towering rowan tree. "There," he said in a whisper. "That's as far as we go today."

Despite her wobbly legs, she objected. "Can't we go a little higher? We must be halfway up the ridge by now."

"More than that." He lay down on the moss and stretched out his legs. "But this is where we stop."

Anna could tell it was pointless to argue. She sighed and lay down on the soft, thick carpet. Her body sank, it seemed, into the ground itself. Eagle hopped off, finding a bed of his own in the tufts.

Then, like the forest around them, they waited in silence.

Chapter 11

FOR SOME TIME ANNA AND SASH lay on their backs in the moss, quiet as the trees themselves. Just watching. One by one, every leaf and needle and twig sparkled with the day's last light, gleamed for a while, then faded into darkness. In the rowan branches above them, the eyes of a nesting thrush glowed an eerie orange.

Anna turned from the deepening shadows to the boy beside her. "Are your, ah . . . people . . . somewhere near?"

"The drumalos are here, all right. But they're waiting. For what comes next." He chortled. "It happens only once a year, on High Hallow Eve. And it's something, I'm sure, no human has ever witnessed."

Until now, thought Anna.

The tension in the air increased. The hair on the back of her neck prickled, and goose bumps swelled on her arms. The sky seemed ready to split open in a storm. But she'd never known a storm like this.

Slowly, the last blush of sunlight disappeared. Anna shivered, and not just from the chilly air. She slid across the moss until her shoulder touched her friend's.

Just then the lowest leaf on the rowan's lowest branch started to quiver. It trembled ever so slightly at first—then faster, and faster. Next more leaves, higher on the tree, started to shake, as if touched by the same swelling wind.

Except there was no wind. Not that Anna could feel, at least.

Like Sash, she sat up, clasping her knees, watching. *What was happening?*

All around them, trees shivered and quaked to the hidden wind. Then came a single, low-pitched note from somewhere in the forest. Like a great wooden horn it blew, with a sound so deep that it shook the very ground. And shook Anna, too, somewhere under her skin.

Another note came—somewhat higher, ringing like a faraway chime. Then another. And another.

Soon a whole chorus filled the air. Blown and bonged and whistled, the notes rang out, echoing from every grove, rolling in a great river of sound. As the notes lifted higher, so did the trees, their boughs raised upward like thousands of arms. And as the notes fell lower, burly roots stirred and dug deeper into the soil.

A new wind gathered, a wind that moved the air as well as the trees. It wailed through the forest, shaking elmwood and oak, hawthorn and beech. Leaves and cones and flakes of bark spun all about. The air smelled of cedar sap and walnut oil. Branches tapped and creaked and shushed, joining with the chorus in one united call.

This was the call of the forest itself—its truest cry, its deepest voice. Anna was sure of it. Aye, this was the voice of the wild woods alive!

She glanced over at Sash, and he met her gaze. His green eyes sparkled as if embedded with stars.

High Hallow Eve had arrived.

Suddenly Anna turned. A face—right there in the bark of the rowan tree beside them! She stared at the face as it sprouted from the trunk. Her whole body tensed. And yet . . . this face looked very different from the one she'd seen before in the forest. This face was round and cheery with huge eyes and a wide, wrinkly mouth. And despite the deepening darkness, the eyes shone with their own inner light, a greenish glow that looked like moonbeams on leaves.

Anna watched, holding her breath. Here was a tree spirit, about to emerge from its home!

The rowan's face bulged outward, swelling like a burl on the trunk. Then came two long-fingered hands, a belly as round as the tree itself, and a pair of bumpy feet. Slowly the figure pulled apart from the trunk, oozing out from the gaps in the bark. Finally, with a moist, sucking sound, it came free.

Standing on his own at last, the fat little fellow raised his arms above his head and started to dance. He slapped his feet on the tree's roots so hard, his round belly jiggled. With a broad wink at Sash, he twirled himself around, howled with joy, then twirled again, faster than before.

All around, spirits emerged from their trees, pulling themselves out of knotholes, through chinks in bark, or up from roots. Right away they, too, started dancing. One elder spirit, as knobby as the old oak where he lived, spun himself in so many circles that he fell to the ground with a thud—and a dizzy grin. Pale-skinned birch spirits threw aside their dangling braids and turned cartwheels and somersaults on the forest floor. Above Anna's head, a thin girl hung with both hands from a branch. She wore a suit of summer grasses that covered even her fingers and toes. As she swung slowly to and fro, her long hair fluttering across her arms, she looked every bit as graceful as a young elm.

Anna didn't know which way to look. It was all so real—yet so amazing.

While the drumalos danced, the strange music swelled even louder. The wind swelled, too, swirling and gusting through the forest. Needles and twigs and leaves filled the air. Everywhere, saplings stomped their roots to the rhythm, while older spirits swayed to each and every note, rowing the air with their branches. And Anna could feel the beat pulsing in her bones.

Someone grabbed Anna's wrist. Sash! He pulled her right into the revelry, whirling her around the rowan. Hands held tight, they jumped and spun and kicked their legs high. Anna threw back her head and laughed—aye, just for the thrill of it all.

"Oh, Sash . . ." She leaped over the shaggy head of a cedar who had sat down to rest. "I love this, I do!"

"Not bad!" he crowed. "With some more practice, you could almost keep up with me."

"Then let's practice all the time!" She smiled as they twirled past a family of elms who were spinning in unison. Here she was, dancing with the very creatures she'd thought were ghouls! "Sash, this is the best day of my life."

"Just wait till tomorrow," he shouted. "When we go up to the willow together. And when you find out—"

"Wait," she interrupted suddenly. Her dancing slowed. "I've been thinking. I want to go up there alone."

"Really?"

"Really. Something tells me it's better that way, just me and the willow. I'm not sure why—just that it's better."

He shook his sandy locks. "Well, all right. But you won't have nearly as much fun without me."

"Aye, that's true." She squeezed his hands. "That's always true."

Just then someone dropped a wreath of white berries on her brow. She let go of Sash and spun around to see who had done it.

Before her stood a gnarled old fellow with a crooked grin. He wore a floppy hat studded with cones. And as he bowed stiffly to Anna, she caught a familiar smell, both tart and sweet.

"Burl!" She threw her arms around the neck of her old friend.

He wrapped his own leathery arms around her, and they started dancing a bouncy sort of jig. "Now there, me girl! *Hoho, hoho.* Methought you might not know me."

"Oh, Burl. I'd always know you!"

He shook his head to the thumping beat, spraying some cones from his hat. "'Tis good to see you so free, me girl."

She whirled herself around, and danced all the faster.

Sash tapped her shoulder. He bowed to Old Burl, then pulled Anna into a new freewheeling frenzy. Her bare feet flew above the ground, hardly touching before they flew again.

Like all the others, they romped long into the night. Sometimes they danced as a pair, and sometimes as part of a long, twisting vine that wound its way among the trees. And sometimes Anna just danced alone, twirling herself around and around in the light of the rising moon.

And when, at last, the festivities ended, she continued to dance in her dreams.

Chapter 15

STILL SWAYING IN HER DREAMS, Anna woke up.

She lay on the bed of moss beneath the rowan. The tree's branches and bark looked normal—no sign that anything unusual had happened. Oh, but she knew better! Twigs and cones jabbed at her back, and crushed berries stuck to her hair. She bent her legs. So sore . . .

Yet she could only smile. What a night she'd known! Stiffly, she sat up and rubbed the bottoms of her feet. Black they were, black as charcoal. And splotched with sap. She pulled a sprig of fern from between her toes, which tickled.

Anna gazed at the sun-shafted woods around her. Leaves, bark, and broken branches lay everywhere, as if a powerful wind had shaken the forest. But she knew well that this had been caused by something much stronger than wind. High Hallow Eve!

And she, herself, had been there.

So had Sash—though she couldn't see him anywhere now. She thought of their flying dance, legs kicking high, and her smile broadened. *And I'll dance with him again, I will.*

She turned toward the higher ground up the slope. *But first . . . the High Willow. I'm going there now. At last.*

She jumped up, despite her sore thighs and calves. Then, like a squirrel, she scampered up the rowan. And peered through the branches toward the ridge. There it was, rising steeply, and closer than ever. And there, at the very top, stood the shape she knew so well. The willow seemed to wave in the wind, beckoning.

But wait! She spied something else, something she hadn't seen before. A cliff, sheer and streaked with water, wrapped around the crest of the ridge. And blocked her way.

Anna stroked her chin. She could go around it, sure. But that would take time—too much time. No, the fastest way to the willow would be to go straight over the cliff.

Down the rowan she scurried. Just as she started off, she heard a squawk from the moss at her feet.

"Eagle!" She stooped and stroked his feathered

head lovingly. "Flying fish eggs, how could I forget you? All that dancing must have rattled my brains."

The bird just tilted his head and glared at her.

"But now we go," she said, half singing. "To the top of the ridge! Oh, what a sight that tree must have been in the wild wind! Now come up here on my shoulder."

Off she tramped up the slope, her feet crunching on chips of bark and twigs. Golden rays drifted through the trees and made pools of shining light on the ground. Bluebells and rosehips quivered in the breeze. Bees hummed above the sweet-smelling grasses.

The forest felt so different today. More . . . friendly. At peace. She pushed the hair back from her forehead. And wondered which had really changed— the forest or herself.

Her steps quickened. What would she find up there? The tree, of course . . . but what else?

She tried to swallow, though her throat felt drier than driftwood. She had to find something! Even something very small. To help her know her own past . . . her own self.

She pushed through some leafy vines that dangled from a hemlock, and stepped over a mesh of fallen trunks. Meanwhile, the land grew steadily steeper.

And dotted with dark boulders—probably broken chunks of the cliff.

Then—a shadow ahead. The cliff itself! She approached and stood beneath it, hands on her hips. Crab claws! It looked awfully sheer, and taller than she'd thought. Water trickled out of the cracks and flowed down the face, making the rock shiny. And, she knew without question, slippery. Very slippery.

"Looks tough, Eagle."

The sparrow made a fierce, sharp whistle.

"Of course I'll be careful, you silly."

She strode over to a deep crack that snaked its way up from the base. Grabbing the edges with her fingers, she pulled herself off the ground. Then she wedged her toes into the crack and crept higher.

Little by little, she climbed. Sometimes she clung mostly to the rock itself, sometimes to the tufts of moss that sprouted from the watery seams. And sometimes, it seemed, to the very air.

As she neared the top of the cliff, the long crack came to a sudden end. What now? She leaned out as far as she dared and scanned the face. There—a thin ledge just to her right. But could she reach it?

She stretched out her hand. Farther . . . and farther . . .

No! Just out of reach.

Anna shook a drop of sweat off her nose. If her hand wouldn't reach, then how about her foot? Clinging tight now with both hands, she lifted one leg. And caught the ledge with her big toe! She wrapped it around the outcropping, braced herself, and—

The lip of rock broke off! She almost fell, but her hands dug deep into their holds and didn't slip. And she listened, heart pounding, as the broken pieces clattered down the cliff.

She steadied herself, despite her sore fingers. And drew an uneven breath. Then, swinging her leg outward again, she caught the ledge at a lower spot.

"Hold tight, Eagle."

Cautiously, she shifted her weight to the ledge. Her hands searched for new holds as she slid herself across the rocky face. Cold, damp rock scraped against her elbows and knees. The muscles in her thighs ached terribly.

Made it! Eagle drummed her shoulder with his foot. She tilted her head and nuzzled him.

The ledge angled upward, and she moved along it briskly. A few moments later, she pulled herself over a gap at the cliff's edge and stood safely on top.

She turned to face the slope above them, densely packed with brambles and trees. She couldn't see the willow, but it couldn't be far. Scratching Eagle's neck feathers, she said, "Almost there, my friend."

Not far up the slope they met a thick stand of hawthorns—so thick, their branches blocked out the sky. Just the same, Anna plunged right in. The wind stirred, and the trees' spicy scent washed over her. To her surprise, the branches seemed to part, their spiky edges swinging away and guiding her through the thicket.

Suddenly she burst out of the branches. Bright sunlight made her squint. But after her eyes adjusted, they opened wider than ever.

For there before her stood the High Willow.

Anna caught her breath. "By the sea and stars . . ."

All alone stood the tree, boughs arching high into the air. And from those limbs hung leaves in long, flowing tresses, a cascade of curtains that nearly touched the ground. The silver-green leaves rippled and swayed with the slightest breeze.

For a long moment, she just stood there, gazing at the tree. Her heart thundered in her chest. And a strange new feeling of warmth flowed through her body.

Her eyes grew misty. She blinked them clear, but more mist came. In a hoarse voice, she spoke to the tree, her moist cheeks shining in the sun.

"Great willow . . . I am Anna." She took a small step closer to the rippling leaves.

The tree's long tresses swayed ever so slightly. They made a soft rustling sound. A sound that soothed, and welcomed. A sound that Anna felt she had heard before, though she couldn't be sure.

Another step closer. "I, well . . . I'm not really sure why I've come. Just that . . . I had to. And that . . ."

She cleared her throat. "I want to find my mother. Or what happened to her. She was here once, wasn't she?"

Her face lowered, and she whispered, "I just want . . . to know her."

A gentle gust stirred the layers of leaves. They seemed to beckon, to call her closer.

Anna stepped among the roots. They felt warm under her feet, and bent ever so slightly with her weight. Welcoming her.

Slowly, she pushed past the leaves. Now she saw the tree's mighty trunk—aye, so thick, it could have been five trunks bound together as one. Sunlight shone on its bark, and shimmered.

She reached for a branch above her head. Sturdy and strong it felt, and just the right height. She smiled to herself. Time to climb this tree! She swung herself up with ease. Whatever else she'd come here for, she wasn't about to miss her chance to climb the highest tree of all.

But something made her pause and go no higher. Something she couldn't quite name. She sat herself on that bottom branch, shrouded by curtains of green, and leaned back against the trunk. *I'm here now. Really here.*

Just at that moment, the wind blew stronger, sweeping through the curtains of leaves. They rustled and billowed outward. The whole tree seemed to draw its own deep breath.

Anna closed her eyes. She felt the willow sway around her, rocking her as she must have been rocked long ago in her mother's arms. These branches held her so gently, so completely. She nestled closer to the tree. Then she heard, in the rustling boughs, a slow, quiet whisper.

Hrraaala lo wwwashhhawaaiii, lo hrraaala wwwashhhalaaaee. Sooohhla shhhowaaa lashh-halooe, heshhhanaala shhhaana shhhooooo.

To Anna, the tree's whisper sounded almost like a

song. And then she remembered her very own words: *A song that blew like the wind, and beat like a—*

"Rowanna! There ye be!"

Master Mellwyn's harsh voice turned her blood to ice. Before she could move, he grabbed her by the leg and yanked her down from the branch. With a thud, she hit the ground. She stared up at his face, twisted by rage and fear.

"Blast, girl, I jest knew I'd find ye here! Now come!" He grabbed hold of her arm. Roughly, he dragged her away from the tree—and back down into the forest.

A shrieking wind struck the ridge. The willow shook wildly, and its tresses snapped like whips. Other trees nearby began to writhe and twist, slashing the air with their branches. Meanwhile, Anna struggled to break free—but the old man's grip only tightened.

"No!" she cried. She beat her fists against his arm and shoulder. "Let me go!"

His eyes seemed to sizzle. "Hush, ye foolish child!"

Brutally, he hauled her along. When they came to the top of the cliff, he veered and dragged her all the way around its side. Then they plunged again down the slope. Eagle tried to cling to her shoulder, but finally tumbled off and landed in a red currant bush.

Anna continued to struggle and shout. When finally she fell to her knees so he couldn't drag her so easily, he whipped off his belt and tied her arms together with a fisherman's knot. Then, shaking his head, he threw her over his shoulder, much as he would a net full of mackerel. He stumbled ahead, back toward the shore.

By now the entire forest was roaring in fury. Trees groaned and smacked their limbs together, showering the old man with leaves, twigs, cones, and other debris. Some branches clawed at his tunic, while others tore loose and slammed to the ground just in front of him. Ghoulish faces appeared in the trunks and burls, glaring angrily.

But Master Mellwyn just wouldn't stop. "I'll not be losin' ye now," he panted over and over. "Not now, or ever."

Chapter 16

AT LAST, AS THE LONG DAY NEARED its end, Master Mellwyn staggered out of the forest and onto the shore. The swollen sun glowed orange on the horizon. All the while, furious winds howled and hurled sand, sticks, and leaves. Behind the old man, the trees slashed the air with their boughs.

He kicked open the cottage door and dropped Anna to the floor. Then, using scattered bits of vine, he lashed her to the main post. She squirmed to break free, though the bindings bit deep into her arms.

"Let me go!" she cried tearfully. "Oh, please, let me go."

"Hush, ye foolish girl," he barked, still panting from the strain of the journey. He slammed the cottage door. "By the plague's own breath! I'm tryin' to save ye! Them ghouls are still a-shriekin' out there." Deep ruts etched his brow. "No tellin' what they'll do next."

"Nothing!" Her voice, sore from shouting, squawked like a wounded gull. "They won't hurt us, I tell you!"

His jaw tightened. "That tree," he spat. "Aye, that's what done this to ye!" He whirled around and threw open the door again. "There be jest one way to stop this. Aye, and stop it forever!"

Bewildered, Anna watched him stomp outside. Then she heard a sound, low and rasping. It rose and fell, rose and fell, like an unending wave on the shore. And though she could barely hear it over the roar of the trees, this was a sound she knew well—the axe being sharpened on the whetstone.

The axe! She shuddered, down to the soles of her feet. For now she grasped his plan. *He's going to chop down the willow.*

"Nooooo!" she howled.

The rasping sound continued.

With all her strength, she tried to break loose. She heaved and tugged. Crab claws! The vines only tightened. The harder she pushed against the post, the more she got splinters in her back and bruises on her ribs.

I've got to get out. Got to!

She twisted again, struggling to pull her arms free.

Sweat, mixed with sap from the forest where she'd danced the night before, dribbled down her brow. She thought of the great willow, standing so high and alone, majestic on the ridge. And the sweeping branches, so like arms, that had held her.

Anna's whole body shook with the strain. Harder she pulled, and harder.

But the vines wouldn't budge.

She slumped back against the post. Her throat swelled, and her sides and shoulders ached. The High Willow . . . felled by the master's axe. And she could do nothing, nothing at all, to stop it.

Rasp, rasp, rasp. Soon he'd be finished. She could almost see the axe slice through the air. And feel its blade bite into the flesh of the tree.

Her tree.

Anna's fists clenched. She must try again!

She braced her feet and pushed back. But instead of ramming into the post as she'd done before, she twisted sideways and leaned hard. Very hard. She put all her weight on the vines, stretching them across the edge of the post. And then she twisted even farther.

The bindings dug into her skin. They creaked and pulled tighter—until one strand suddenly burst apart. She freed one arm, tore off the vines, and stood again.

Anna rubbed her sore arms and started for the door. She had to steal that axe somehow!

Just as she reached for the latch, she caught herself. No—she'd never overpower the master. Better to creep past him and dash into the forest. Then she could get help. From Sash, from anyone she could find. Mayhaps the tree spirits themselves.

Carefully, she opened the door a crack. She could see the master, standing over the whetstone, his back to the cottage. Scarlet rays from the setting sun washed over the beach and the trees beyond.

She pushed on the door. It creaked a bit, but the sound was lost in the angry wail of the trees and the ongoing grind of the whetstone. The master didn't look up.

As softly as a windblown seed, Anna slipped outside. She stepped over Old Burl's roots and hid behind the trunk. The instant she touched the fir's bark, she felt a shiver—whether her own or the tree's, she couldn't tell.

She chewed her lip, watching the master, waiting for the right moment to run. He'd be done any second now. At last, she saw him pause to check the blade. Now!

She bolted for the forest. Suddenly, before she had crossed the sand—

"Anna!" The voice came from the brambles at the edge of the trees. "Over here!"

Sash! The boy waved at her, his hair flapping in the wind. Eagle watched, perched on his shoulder.

The old man spun around. Seeing Anna, he cursed, "Bones! Ye'll be the death of me, ye will!"

Just then he caught sight of the figure in the brambles. His lip curled in rage. "A ghoul! See there—them horrid fangs and claws? Jest waitin' to get us." He raised the axe. "Stand back, girl!"

"No!" shouted Anna above the screaming wind. "He's no ghoul! He's—"

"Out of me way, ye fool." The sharpened blade flashed in the sunset light. Before she could cut him off, he lunged straight at Sash. "Now death to ye, ghoul!"

Suddenly his foot caught on one of Burl's roots. He sprawled forward, slammed hard into the trunk, and fell on his side.

"Quick now!" called Sash. "Let's go."

Anna ran to her friend, clearing the brambles in one leap. She started to follow him into the trees—

when she heard a groan from behind. She stopped and glanced back at the beach.

The master lay still on the sand. Blood soaked his tunic over his ribs. He'd fallen on the axe!

Weakly, he rolled onto his back. He tried to sit up, as his knobby fingers clutched his wounded side. Blood seeped down his wrist and forearm. He groaned again, then sank back to the ground.

"Come, Anna!" cried Sash. "Into the forest! This is your chance."

Her feet turned toward the trees. But her gaze wouldn't leave the wounded man. She watched as he lifted his head again.

Their eyes met, and he scowled. "Leave me, ye wretched beast!" His head fell back with a thud.

"Come on!" Sash stomped hard on the ground. "Anna, what are you doing?"

For a few more seconds, she watched the blood ooze from the gash. The master just glared back at her. "Get out o' me sight," he hissed. "Go! Away with ye!"

At last, Anna turned her face to the forest. She was free now, she knew it. Free to go to the ridge. To the willow.

And yet . . . She glanced back at the old man.

Biting her lip, she faced the forest again. Then she ran to Sash's side—and right past him. All the way to the glade she raced, as the boy trotted behind. At the great beech, she veered to the far side of the clearing and stopped at a black alder sapling. The same sapling Sash had once used to stem her own bleeding, from her own gash.

She broke off a twig, then turned to her friend. "You chew this first?"

He sighed, reading her thoughts. "Yes, but only the bark." He took her hand. "When will you come back?"

She swallowed. "I don't know." With that, she pulled away and dashed back to the shore.

Chapter 17

T HE BLACK ALDER BARK DID ITS part. But saving Master Mellwyn took much more than that.

After Anna managed to drag the old man's limp body into the cottage, her real work began. For three whole days she washed his wound with salt water, made poultices from pads of kelp, spooned liquids down his throat, and sang to him softly. Blood stained his straw pallet on the floor, and much of the cottage besides.

Finally, he opened his eyes. And when he did, those eyes nearly popped with amazement.

"Ye came . . . ," he began, then licked his dry lips. "Ye came back?"

Anna merely nodded while she laid a fresh poultice on his skin. Then she turned him onto his side, wrapped a bandage around his ribs, and rolled him back. Eagle, seated at the edge of the pallet, gave a cluck of approval.

She sang for a while, a song about skin torn apart, and starting to mend. About bones as sturdy as tree trunks, and bendable as saplings. And about a darkened glade in the forest, struck by a sudden shaft of light, warm and healing.

The man listened, his face paler than sun-bleached bones. He placed a trembling hand on her own. "Ye sing pretty, child."

"Hush now, you need to rest."

He shook his head. "And ye saved me, child. Stopped me bleedin'."

"No," she replied, "the alder bark did that."

He caught his breath. "Ye used . . . a *tree*?"

"Aye, a tree." She faced him squarely. "And I learned how to do it from someone you called a ghoul."

His whole body stiffened.

"But really," she went on, "he's a tree spirit."

The old man shuddered. And then he rasped, "There be somethin' . . . I needs to say."

"Not now. You're too weak." She leaned over to the hearth and tossed a slab of driftwood on the coals. A splash of sparks lit the room.

He waved his hand before her face. "Listen, child! Ye must . . . hear this story."

"What story?"

"The one ye've asked me to tell afore." He tried to clear his throat. "It's time ye finally hear . . . jest how I found ye. Long ago, in the forest."

Anna's eyebrows jumped. "Tell me. Please." She squatted lower, as the sparrow hopped to her side.

The old man turned aside. Firelight played on the back of his head. He was gazing, it seemed, not at the rough-hewn table, or at the cottage wall, but at something else. Something far beyond that wall, far beyond that place and time.

"Years ago, ye see, I be livin' . . . a long way from here. On the other side of yon ridge. I be a village smith, forgin' tools for jest about any use. And Rowanna . . ."

He looked at her for a long moment. "I be . . . a happier man. There be a woman, me wife."

Anna started. "Was she—"

"No, no, listen! There be me wife—and also our daughter, our own little girl. She be small, jest a babe . . . but she already be a singer. And one day, I could tell, a dancer. For she be blessed, aye, with a dancer's spirit."

He worked his tongue. "Until . . ."

"Until what?"

"The plague!" He spat the words. "The killin' plague. It came with no warnin'—and took them both." His eyes closed for a few seconds. "And so I fled. From the sickness, aye, but more so from the memory. Fled across the fields and hills, jest tryin' to get away."

She touched his brow, as rumpled as the bark of an old oak.

A sound—part sob, part sigh—burst from his throat. "She be me only child, Rowanna! All I ever had. I held her, tight in me arms, right till she died. But I couldn't save her. Couldn't keep her tiny breaths a-comin'."

Her eyes, like his, grew clouded. Hearth coals glowed in them, like sunlight through mist.

"And so . . . I climbed yon ridge up there. 'Twas the highest place I could find. I be thinkin' I'd hurl meself off a cliff right then. Aye, and end that cursed memory."

His voice suddenly quieted. "But there I found . . . a tree. Yer precious willow. And there, restin' among its roots, be a bright and smilin' babe. 'Twas ye, girl! And a true enough miracle it was."

Anna tried to swallow.

"And there be a greater miracle yet, Rowanna!

When I looked at yer face, gazin' up from the ground, ye looked . . ." His words trailed off as he studied her closely. "Like me own daughter! Like the face, in all this world, I most wanted to see."

Anna tilted her head. *Like the face I most wanted to see.* Something about those words sounded familiar. But what?

"So then," she asked, "what happened?"

His brow furrowed. "I . . . well, I took ye into me arms. Jest to hold ye one more time, ye see? Not to . . ." He swallowed hard. "Then suddenly the willow's branches started grabbin' at me, tearin' at me face and arms! Like it come all alive. And angry! I saw a face—aye, a horrid face—right there in the branches. Like it be pullin' itself right out of the very bark!"

He stared at her with haunted eyes. "That ghoul be wantin' ye, child—wantin' us both. But I wasn't goin' to lose ye! Not again! So I held ye tight and ran. Through that whole horrid forest I ran, trees a-clutchin' at me and clawin' me face and crashin' down near on top of me. Aye, and I didn't stop runnin' till I got all the way here—to this very strip of sand. And here I made our home."

The old man peered at her. "I saved ye, see? From

the ghouls! And yet . . . it didn't seem right somehow. Almost like . . ."

She leaned close. "What?"

"Like I was stealin' somebody else's child."

Somebody else's . . .

All at once, Anna understood. Her heart vaulted in her chest. "I am the willow's child!" she cried aloud. "And she . . . is my mother."

The old man gazed up at her. "So," he said at last, "you are truly—"

"A tree spirit."

Gently, she slid her fingers into his own. Fingers that took the shape he so wanted to see. Fingers of a human girl.

Then Anna lifted her hand, seeing it truly for the first time. It looked as slender as a willow shoot. And bent so easily! Her knuckles poked out like knots on a branch. And her skin—so wonderfully brown, with flecks of green.

"Ye will . . . be leavin' me, then?"

She nodded. "Aye. But you will always know where I am. And sometimes, when the breeze is strong, you might still hear my songs on the wind."

The next morning, Anna changed his bandage for the last time, then helped him into his chair. She kissed his brow, put Eagle on her shoulder, and stepped over to the door. Before she lifted the latch, though, she stopped.

For a moment, she gazed around the cottage— at the thatch above her head, the stones of the hearth, the straw where she'd spent so many nights. And at the old man who sat there, just watching her go.

And then she opened the door. Anna stepped outside, and into the waiting arms of the trees.

Chapter 18

HIGH ON THE RIDGE THAT CROWNS that forest by the sea, a pair of willow trees stand. One of them, gnarled with age, stretches her boughs skyward. And the other, a young sapling, grows nearby in a place of her own.

The two trees stand apart, even as they grow together. Their highest limbs meet and make an archway of leaves. They are touched by the same winds, and by the same light of sun, moon, and stars.

Sometimes, a sand-colored bear cub visits the sapling. He nuzzles the nest of the sparrow who lives there. But mostly he just plays in the branches. He hangs in them, swings in them, and swats them—until the branches swat back.

And sometimes, that bear is joined by another—a brown bear who romps through the forest with her friend. Who races through the sunlit groves, always ready to wrestle. And who loves nothing more than to climb a tree.

Whenever breezes sweep across the ridge, the two willows weave and sway as one. Their leafy boughs, falling like tresses by their sides, move in a dreamlike dance. And while the willow trees dance, they make a song all soft and slow and whispery.

A song that blows like the wind, and beats like a heart.